THE
TAKUS
ICED FIRE

JOE LIVINGSTON

AuthorHouse™ UK
1663 Liberty Drive
Bloomington, IN 47403 USA
www.authorhouse.co.uk
Phone: 0800 047 8203 (Domestic TFN)
+44 1908 723714 (International)

Because of the dynamic nature of the Internet, any web addresses or links contained in this book may have changed
since publication and may no longer be valid. The views expressed in this work are solely those of the author and do not
necessarily reflect the views of the publisher, and the publisher hereby disclaims any responsibility for them.

Any people depicted in stock imagery provided by Getty Images are models,
and such images are being used for illustrative purposes only.
Certain stock imagery © Getty Images.

This book is printed on acid-free paper.

ISBN: 978-1-7283-9874-7 (sc)
ISBN: 978-1-7283-9873-0 (e)

Print information available on the last page.

Published by AuthorHouse 03/09/2020

authorHOUSE®

The Takus
Iced Fire

Joe Livingston

Inhabitants of Esterevania

<u>The Tardan Bukai</u>

- Wok – Leader
- Wasul – Potion maker
- Tekir – Wise, old advisor
- Orsov – Army commander
- Eli
- Erith – Wife of Orsov
- Yond
- Zoltan

- Tak – Noron species
- Revar – Noron species

<u>The Tardan Rhakta</u>

- Thori – Leader
- Zak
- Rostia– Female
- Zarov
- Urshu

- Lato – Noron species
- Wantu – Noron species

<u>The Sheerak</u>

- Salak – Leader
- Golo
- Etar
- Nepht
- The scout - Grapite
- Sal, son of Salak
- Kandor

<u>The Burabob</u>

- Gux
- Baba

<u>Lome</u>

- Supreme Undersea Leader

Fire and Ice cannot be joined
Either the Fire dies, or the Ice melts .

Chapter 1

THE FINAL TARDAN BATTLE

Lato stood in the freezing cold, waiting anxiously to try his new destructive invention. He nestled his smooth and slender humanoid cheek against the transparent barrel of the shiny new projectile launcher. His binocular eyes narrowed as he monitored the advancing Bukai Tardan tribe through the viewfinder. He suddenly remembered the vivid dream he had experienced only days before.

"Mm, must refocus," he muttered.

He could see his enemy clearly, but he patiently waited for the perfect shot. The shape of the Tardan men was familiar to him, as he lived with Tardan people himself, but Lato belonged to the rival Rhakta tribe. He looked down at their stocky, short, hairy bodies as they made tactical advances through the icy valley. Their long rabbit-like ears waved in the cold winds. Lato was not Tardan; he was Noron. a humanoid from the North of Esterevania. The Noron people were twice the height of the Tardan, with a lean and slender physique and smooth, hairless skin. Lato had to crouch down low behind a snow-covered rock to avoid being spotted; his elongated legs were bent in the most uncomfortable position. Comfort was not the priority, though; victory was. His Rhakta tribe had been bitter rivals of the Bukai for generations, and the resentment ran deep. The original cause of their mutual hatred seemed irrelevant now. Each battle had its own cause, and the result was always a massive loss of life, usually on both sides. This time would be no different. That was just the way of life of Esterevania.

Lato noticed a gap in their front line of warriors and seized the opportunity. With his delicate fingers, he pressed the trajectory sequence button, which instantly activated the launch. He held his breath and watched intently as the projectile hurtled towards its intended victims. It took mere seconds but felt like a life time to Lato as he waited to see the true destructive power of his new weapon.

On contact, it ripped open a Bukai warrior, his small squat body smashed against the valley wall. Lato cheered.

"Perfect, absolutely perfect!"

He knew that his Tardan leader, Thori, would be pleased and this gave him great personal satisfaction. The Noron people lived with the Tardans in both tribes; they were far more intelligent than their comrades but never sought power. Instead they were satisfied in their respected and integral roles as inventors. They were able to use their superior intellect to improve the quality of life of the Tardan people. Of course in the volatile and violent world they lived in, they also used their skills and intelligence to create destructive weaponry. To the Noro's, though, the use to which their inventions might be put did not concern them. They measured their success only on the achievement of their goals. Morality was not an issue.

This latest if not greatest battle had been the result of an accident just a day before. A scouting party from the Bukai tribe had strayed on to the ancient burial ground of their Tardan enemy. These sacred grounds were nestled between two giant glaciers, and despite their apparent ignorance of the exact location, the Rhakta lookouts didn't spare even a moment's thought before attacking the Bukai, who had not expected violence that day and were utterly destroyed. One survivor, though badly wounded, managed to escape, dragging his small torn body through vast, undulating ice formations to alert Wok, his Bukai leader, to the attack. Another fierce battle between the Tardan rival tribes was now inevitable.

The Rhakta had chosen the superior high ground of the Nardi glacier. It was only two kilometres from their underground city and was well known by their people.

The Bukai chose to position themselves at the bottom of two sloped ridges, on either side of a narrow corridor which led into and faced the Nardi valley and glacier. The Bukai faction were clearly at a disadvantage with their position, but their leader was confident of success. Wok knew that his tribe had the upper hand: they had a new invention that was like nothing any Tardan had ever seen before. The new Bukai weapon was called a Takus, in honour of its inventor, Tak a Bukai Noron.

What made the Takus special was its multitude of uses. Unlike a simple projectile launcher, it did more than just rip apart the enemy—it could turn around an entire battle. The Takus could break through ice with its huge rotating blades, twenty feet in diameter. It had the potential to cut into the side of a glacier to create protective caves anywhere. The Bukai would no longer be restricted by the lay of the land; they could manipulate their environment to create their own fate. These blades could also fold back to reveal large, tough discs with electronic "eyes" positioned on and around the circumference. These eye' were linked to a light sensor and could be easily preset to fire a fusillade of laser beams within a sixteen-kilometre radius.

The warriors of the Bukai tribe wore close-fitting steel-mesh armour. Each regiment of the large army had its own designated flag and colour. They advanced in perfect formation like ocean waves of destruction, stealthily moving their ice machines and laser weapons through the valley. The Rhakta tribe wore thick, black, reinforced leather amour, complete with modest bronze fittings. The leather was plain, with the sole purpose of protection.

As the two tribes settled into their positions and nightfall fell, a blizzard swept in from the north. As the freezing temperatures took hold, both tribes knew they needed to take shelter and rest before the battle that awaited them the following day.

CHAPTER 2

THE BUKAI TRIBE TAKES SHELTER

Wok, the Bukai leader, ordered his commander, Orsov, to make a shelter within the glacier. Before today, this would have been a mammoth mission. But now the Bukai tribe had the Takus machine.

Orsov detailed Eli and Revar, his friends and comrades, to assist him. Eli was a Tardan, and Revar was Noron. Despite their obvious physical and intellectual differences, they worked well together. Wok and the chief designer, Tak, looked on. They were confident in the abilities of the Takus, but even they were impressed at the speed and relentless manner in which it burrowed into sheer ice. The large, comfortable ice shelter was complete in moments. The Tardans and Norons stood side by side to admire it.

"It is an incredible machine," Orsov said, shaking his head in disbelief.

"Of course it is," Tak said with a laugh. "Did you doubt its capabilities?"

"I must admit," Orsov said with a smile, "the sheer size of it did make me doubtful."

Wok ordered the elite first and second battalions of his army to take shelter first. He detailed Orsov to create enough shelters to accommodate the rest of the Bukai tribe. A total of six were completed within the hour, including one for Wok to stay in alone. The whole army were safe, warm, and dry on both ridges. Everyone began to settle in for the night.

Wok summoned his chief Norons, Tak and Revar, along with Orsov. As they entered his cave, he greeted them with a big smile, his jagged teeth gleaming and his small hairy face wrinkling around the eyes. He stroked his long ears with his small, soft, shaggy hands and then rubbed his shiny breastplate—a sign of authority in the Bukai.

"Tonight", he announced, rubbing his paws together, "we will toast to Noron genius. The Takus has sheltered my army from the extreme cold, enabling us to rest and prepare for battle. This is something we should celebrate." Wok picked up a large clay jug of red wine that had been produced at the vineyards in their underground city.

"Drink," ordered Wok as Orsov poured the wine into four small clay goblets. "Tonight we rest our bodies and minds. We will need all our strength to defeat the Rhakta tribe tomorrow."

As the Norons sipped their wine, they both felt deep satisfaction. They couldn't help but look around the crystal ice cavern and feel immense pride, knowing full well that the Bukai Tardans would have been unable to achieve this without their help.

The wine began to take effect, and the small band of Bukai leaders huddled together beside the campfire at the far end of the cave. The alcohol coursed through their veins, and they began to talk more freely.

"Maybe one day", pondered Wok, "the Tardan people will live as one nation and not as separate tribes at war. I am getting tired of the continuous fighting. I think we should start paying more attention to the teachings of the ancients."

"The ancients?" Tak asked.

"They had a system", Wok explained, "that allowed them to work together. Anyone who went against the law was simply banished. It sounds harsh, but it worked."

"It does seem like an effective way to make sure everyone complies," Orsov said with a sarcastic smile.

"It would be tense, I am sure." Wok laughed. "But I bet there would be less war and death in comparison with how we live now."

"Tak and Revar are the direct descendants of the banished ancients, isn't that right?" Orsov asked, gesturing at the Noron members of the group. They both smiled and nodded in acknowledgement.

"Well, maybe you are the cause of all our strife," said Wok sternly. The atmosphere felt as if it had been sucked out of the cave. The group held their breath in anticipation. But after a few seconds, Wok burst into laughter, and the others joined in immediately, relieved. Wok may have been in a good mood on this night, but they were all aware how his mood could change quickly over seemingly trivial comments.

Silence fell again as the impending battle weighed on the group. Orsov stared at his flickering shadow on the wall and thought about his pregnant wife, Erith. She had begged him to stay, but as Wok's commander he knew he had no choice in the matter. Despite his lack of control, he had promised his wife it would be the last time. He hoped with all his heart that he would come home to her and their unborn child and that it would indeed be the last battle. He doubted it very much, though, and this thought was sobering.

In the silence Wok was also retrospective, he knew he was a good leader to the Bukai, he was well respected and his warriors followed him into battle without question. Although he knew deep down that they had little choice, it still made him feel important. He was normally so aloof, even with his own trusted commanders and inventors. Tonight though he had let his guard down and it felt good.

"What a shame," Tak interrupted everyone's thoughts "that it takes impending battle for us to come together like this." Wok looked at Tak with an apologetic expression; it was as if he had been reading his mind.

The evening continued and the group turned their attention to battle plans for the following day. The camp fire flame burned low and the vibrant dancing shadows on the cave wall slowly diminished until they were virtually gone.

Eventually, Wok ordered everyone to bed; he led the way, scurrying on all fours towards the cave entrance. Orsov followed in the same fashion, the Noron humanoids stretched their long limbs, brushing off the fragments of ice that had fallen from the cave roof in the heat of the fire. Their Tardan counterparts were only hip high when standing next to the Noron's. As they reached the cave opening Wok stopped and waited for the others to reach him. He grabbed Tak's smooth hand.

"Victory will be ours. You have given me the will and ability to win." He gestured to the rest of his inner circle, "Tonight, you have all shown me the benefit of being more open and allowing myself to become closer to my people. I feel like we, as Tardan and Noron people, are ready to change for the better. I will not forget this night my friends."

They all nodded and smiled, feeling slightly uncomfortable by Wok's change in persona. It was however, a welcome relief.

"We will meet tomorrow before dawn as Orsov has suggested" Wok continued "to finalise the battle plans with sober minds." As they stepped outside they noticed the snow had ceased and the bright pink Esterevania winter night sky lit up the ridge like the glow from hot steel.

Wok shook hands with each of his warriors as they left and he returned to his cave. Orsov went towards his sleeping quarters and the Noron went together towards theirs.

"Our leader has shown good sense tonight," commented Revar. "So many of the Bukai have become suspicious of him recently"

"I imagine this new attitude will be received well" said Tak in agreement as the Noron pair entered their dimply lit cave. Before they retired, Tak told the cave guard to ensure that everyone was awake before dawn. There were many preparations to make before the battle.

CHAPTER 3

THE RHAKTA CAMP TAKES SHELTER

As soon as he had heard about the killing of one of the scouting party, Thori, the Rhakta leader had moved with the utmost urgency. Thori and his army had travelled the short distance to the Nardi Glacier on foot. They wore specially made ice boots with spiked soles that helped them to cross the sloping ice with ease. Their army formations were completely different to the organised colour coded regiments of the Bukai. Instead Thori's entire army were divided into three large units.

The first unit contained the battle weapons and operators who were mostly Noron. The second was the largest with close to 5,000 warriors fully dressed in their thick black leather battle gear. Finally the third unit was mobile; it was the unit that Thori and his closest commanders travelled in. The third unit rode on the muscular backs of huge, tusked polar bears that had specifically trained for battle. The bears wore leather seats, matching the uniform of their riders. The stark colour difference between their fur and the leather made them stand out against the white snow. The Tardan's steered their bears with long reins which were tied to each side of a face muzzle. The polar bears were able to transport the Tardan Bukai leaders at great speed which had proven essential in battle many times before.

As they trudged onwards, Thori glanced at his caged rabbits which were being carried alongside him by a fellow warrior's polar bear. They were unsettled because of the movement and the noise of the chanting Rhakta tribe but Thori wouldn't be without them. They were his beloved pets and he hoped their presence would bring him luck in battle. He glanced at Zarov, the bird trainer who carried the black rooks on his back. The giant and majestic birds had been specially trained to carry messages in battle and were well accustomed to the sounds, smells and sights of Tardan war. Thori loved his animals. They represented a peace and innocence that he admired.

Each warrior had a three foot long projectile missile launcher that glistened in the Esterevanian sun. Additionally, some of the warriors carried curved sabres for hand to hand combat. There were also three jet powered rocket launchers each needing six strong Tardan men to haul them over the ice. The efficiency and accuracy of these rocket launchers was still something the Noron's in the Rhakta debated over but they were powerful weapons and today, power was essential. The launchers and rockets were positioned at each end and directly behind where they planned to dig the main troop trenches. The three unit army had taken only an hour to get into their battle positions.

Thori had placed his army in the best possible location knowing full well that his warriors would be spotted by the enemy. Thori wanted to intimidate his Tardan enemy.

Being so open about his army's position was taking a risk and he knew it. Even though they had the high ground they were still visible and therefore vulnerable. Thori also knew that the Bukai would be forced into setting up camp in the narrow corridor of the valley; they would have been foolish to amass any closer to the Rhakta warriors and if Thori knew Wok at all, he knew he was not foolish.

They spent the day digging trenches along the half mile sloped glacier. They covered the outer edges of the trenches with blocks of hard snow. This gave the Rhakta men comfortable movement within their camp, protection from the blizzard and also enabled them to see the two ridged corridor of the Nardi Valley. The Rhakta tribe now felt safe and secure in the seemingly impenetrable location on top of the Nardi glacier. Although they were somewhat exposed to the elements they had prepared well.

In any event, the Tardan bodies were designed to cope with the extreme weather; their skin was covered in a thick coarse fur and under their skin they were well insulated with a healthy layer of fat. Their hands and feet were small which also stopped excess heat loss. The Noron on the other hand were very different and relied on thick animal fur clothing to keep out the freezing temperatures. Their elongated fingers and toes had to be covered well to avoid frost bite.

As they were finishing off the trenches, Zak, a trusted warrior of Thori's approached him smiling.

"We have done well Sir" he said, "we shall see what the Bukai are made of now"

"Our warriors are in great spirits and it's good to see." Thori replied gleefully.

The Noron called Lato and his assistant Wantu approached.

"This Noron man has once again proved his worth to us all" Thori said encouragingly patting Lato on the lower back, as it was the highest his arm would reach.

"I am pleased to be of service to you Thori" said Lato, "I sometimes think about how far the Noron's have come over the generations. It wasn't so long ago that the Tardan people completely distrusted us and now here we are, making weapons for you!" Wantu nodded in sober agreement as if he himself had experienced the banishment and loneliness of his ancestors.

"There is still some distrust." Wantu added cautiously. "Even though I have lived and worked among Tardan's my entire life I know that some of them still dislike Noron men."

"Really?" Thori asked in astonishment. "I had no idea any of my people would discriminate against the Noron people. You have done so much for us and our community. You must tell me who they are; I will not have you disrespected." Lato responded, " My prophetic dream, confirmed that Wantu, but It is pointless to bring this up really," Lato said disapprovingly glancing at Wantu. "It will only cause more friction. We Noron do not focus on the negative; we focus only on our objectives and the desire to achieve positive results. Your acceptance of us is enough."

"Well" said Thori, clearly embarrassed, "If any of the Tardan's disrespect you in any way, be sure to let me know." He turned to his Rhakta warriors within hearing distance.

"I hope you all heard that" he boomed "be sure to pass the message on to your comrades. The Noron's are not to be disrespected in any way. Is that understood?" The Tardan's surrounding Thori had instinctively stopped their work and stood to attention listening to their leader.

"Yes sir," they all said in automatic unity.

"Now that is said, I want you all to retire and sleep peacefully tonight. Pray to our great god Kuba who will give us strength for the battle ahead."

The warriors of the Rhakta tribe went to bed in their trenches and said their prayers, confident in their god, their leader and the morning's victory. They all slept well.

CHAPTER 4

THE BUKAI CAMP – MORNING OF THE BATTLE

The distant sound of trumpets woke Tak up. He immediately sat bolt upright, quickly getting to his feet and heading towards the cave entrance. He must have been sleeping in a state of awareness, ready to act spontaneously if needed. It was before sunrise but as he looked out he could see rows upon rows of camp fires on the ridge above.

"There are so many Rhakta," Tak said to the cave guard with concern etched in his voice. "I think it is time we woke everyone up. Get to work," he ordered. The guard set about evacuating the caves.

Orsov had also been woken by the trumpet noise and had been spurred into action. He was rounding up the warriors himself, feeling fresh and ready for battle, adrenalin running through his veins.

Revar, Orsov and Tak met together in the middle of the caves, the air was cold and still. They summoned the regiment and battle leaders. Under darkness, as the first signs of morning began encroaching, the small group discussed their action plans for the day ahead.

"It is obvious," said Orsov "that the Rhakta do not know our exact position therefore we must move our troops as far up the sloped ridges as possible."

"Good plan," Revar added, "the range of our laser hand guns is only half a mile so the closer we can get the better."

"What about protection for our front lines?" asked one of the front line battalion leaders, "as we move up the ridge, we will surely be vulnerable?"

"Don't worry," assured Orsov. "We shall move the Takus machine to the front. The large titanium discs should give you all plenty of protection as well as unique fire power."

"What about the middle and rear of the main columns?" asked another battalion leader.

"The Vanadium Arm Shields that Tak and I have designed," said Revar proudly, "can be held above the heads of each warrior. It will be as effective as covering our men in a huge armoured blanket."

"Keep your troops calm," Warned Orsov, "It is a dangerously high ridge and our men are not used to such heights in battle; panic could result in defeat!"

"Well, are we ready?" The group turned to the gruff commanding voice approaching and saw Wok. His brown hair was carefully groomed and looked shiny and smooth, he was fitted with protective armour and his breast plate shone like gleaming stars .

"Almost," assured Orsov before continuing his conversation. "How strong are these Vanadium Arm shields then?" he asked Tak and Revar "If you want them to be held over our warriors heads, can you be absolutely sure they will be able to withstand direct laser contact?"

"Yes we are," said Tak confidently, with a slight air of arrogance.

"We have tested them extensively with our own lasers and they were more than sufficient," assured Revar.

Wok stroked his long drooping ears deep in thought, "It is a pity the ice formation on either side of the Nardi valley is so thick. It would have been a fantastic ambush opportunity but we will never be able to get up there."

"Well, don't give up on the idea just yet;" teased Revar, "I have noticed an area near the top of both of the ridges that may be of use for us. I cannot be sure though. A scouting party will have to be sent during the battle to inspect it."

The group looked at Revar; puzzled by his cryptic comment.

"I will tell you later," laughed Revar, enjoying the power of knowledge over the others. "I do not want to arouse any undue optimism until I hear the scouting party report."

"You Noron's are always so secretive with your scheming plans and ideas," laughed Orsov.

Wok didn't like being kept in the dark but he trusted Revar implicitly and if he had a reason to be secretive, he respected that. He had also made a promise to himself last night that he would listen to his men closely and be more open himself. It wouldn't have been a good start if he demanded Revar's compliance before sunrise.

"Right then" Wok distracted everyone's thoughts from the Revar mystery, "we must get organised. Orsov, you will lead the right column of Bukai warriors and I will take the left. We have only moments before dawn."

"Yes sir." they all replied in unison, standing a little straighter as they spoke. They went their separate ways with their individual tasks in mind.

The Bukai worked hard, the machines were eased up the ridges and the operators were positioned in their small elevated seats inside. They were dwarfed by the huge tracks which clung noisily to the iced ridge. They rumbled onwards until Orsov ordered them to stop.

Everything was ready.

CHAPTER 5

FIGHTING COMMENCES

Orsov had been told by Wok to wait for his laser gun signal before moving forward any more. When Wok understood that everyone was ready, he wasted no time in promptly firing his laser, sending a beam upward towards the ever growing bright sky of the Esterevania dawn. Orsov immediately climbed up the rear stairway of Takus 1 to the small elevated platform so he could address his comrades. His long ears flapped in the wind as he tugged nervously at his meshed armour.

"We are ready to claim victory over our Tardan enemy" he shouted in the most commanding voice he could muster. The Tardan Bukai army went wild, beating their chest armour, waving their shields in the air and making deep, short gruff noises; the battle call of the Bukai tribe. As their shields were waved high they caught the reflection of the Esterevania sun that had started to peak above the glacier, forming a mirage effect of shimmering steel.

"Keep your body well protected," Orsov warned when the hysteria had died down, "Remember, the Rhakta tribe have powerful weapons, but so do we! We will win!"

The hysteria started again as the warriors chanted;

"Bukai! Bukai! Bukai!"

Thori the Rhakta leader had heard the rumble of the mysterious Takus machines as the Bukai had moved both of them into place. He had swiftly finished his own preparations by moving his army into their battle positions. Lato and Wantu were ready on the left side trenches which faced the south of the valley. It was while moving the launchers into place that Lato saw a gap in the shielded barrier of Orsov's unit. He wasted no time in launching the first strike of the day; it pierced through the gap of shields and tore apart a dozen of the Bukai men.

The shot came as a shock to Orsov, although he was ready for battle he hadn't expected such a devastating beginning to the combat.

"Direct the laser– 90 degrees North East," he screamed, "let's take that Rhakta weapon down!"

The large Takus burrowing blades fell back ominously revealing the laser disc. After a quick computer adjustment the operator pressed the attack button and a huge fiery circle of laser beams enveloped Lato's rocket launcher; completely destroying it.

Despite Lato's weapon being devastated Wantu and Lato escaped unharmed by taking cover in the trench. Lato peeped up from their hiding place at the charred remains of his launcher.

"I had no idea the Rhakta weapons were so dangerous" he said to Wantu with a worried look on his face.

Wantu nodded, "How do we stop such a machine?" he asked.

Lato sat back, behind him in the trench was one of the cages which held a black rook inside. The loud squawking sound made him jump. He stroked his chin with his long humanoid fingers.

"I've got an idea," he exclaimed. "We will send a message to Thori telling him to aim all the rocket launchers at the Bukai laser machine. They must all aim and fire at the same time to stand any chance of destroying it."

Wantu agreed this was their only chance; there was no time for further discussion. He immediately wrote out a coded message and then despatched the large rook to Thori's trench position.

The rook took off, its 12 foot wing span forming a majestic outline on the horizon as it glided towards Thori with trained accuracy. The dangerous talons of the rook spread apart as it landed near Thori instantaneously releasing the message.

As Thori read it, his bearded face twisted with determination.

"We must destroy the two Bukai laser machines," he commanded, "We need to aim our remaining rocket launchers at them now!"

His warriors followed their leader's instructions. The two rocket launcher operators pointed their weapons towards Takus 1. They set the computer and each paused with their hairy stubby fingers ready to press the attack button.

"Fire!" shouted Thori.

There was a sudden tremendous roar accompanied by a blinding flash as the rockets pounded towards Takus 1, each missed their intended target but hit the glacier behind. A huge explosion erupted; splintered pieces of jagged ice tore into the Bukai warrior column.

Orsov screamed in anguish as one of his Bukai friends, decapitated and mangled, disappeared over the ridge.

"Reassemble the column" he shouted to Revar. "We must keep going."

Revar focused on his instructions, trying to block out the screams that still echoed across the valley as the Bukai warriors continued to die in agony; plummeting to their death and bleeding from horrific injuries.

On the opposite ridge, Wok watched the devastation caused to Orsov's regiment. He ordered his machine operator to aim at the Rhakta rocket launchers that had caused such destruction to his men. Takus 2 spun around threateningly.

"Fire! Fire! Fire!" shouted Wok impatiently.

The Takus erupted with a merciless bombardment. The beams honed in on the Rhakta rocket launcher with incredible accuracy. It was instantly obliterated, sending metal components skywards like a giant fire cracker.

Thori was in deep trouble; two of the rocket launchers were now destroyed, leaving only one at the back of his central trenches. He screeched at Zak;

"We must move the remaining rocket launcher to a safe position. Take the men you need and move it to the back of the slopes. I want it in a direct line with the Bukai positions. They have the more powerful weapons; our only chance will be to surprise them."

"But that rocket launcher is protecting our whole rear flank," argued Zak.

Thori replied with a strong sense of authority; "I am sorry Zak, this is the best move for the overall battle. Tell the warriors at the western flank to direct and fire their projectiles simultaneously at the Bukai laser, that should offer them some protection before we destroy the machine."

Zak accepted Thori's explanation and despite his reservation, decided not to argue with his leader. He quickly selected six troops to help him with their attack, and together they mounted upon their tusked polar bears. They bounded off at great speed towards the western flank to follow Thori's instructions.

When the last rocket launcher was in the right place, Zak explained Thori's plan to Lato.

"We must fire all our weapons simultaneously at the Bukai machine."

"It's the only way." agreed Lato. "Tell the warriors in the trenches to hold fire until I give the signal." Zak left and whilst heading back to Thori's position, he shouted Lato's message to the troops in the trenches.

Meanwhile, unbeknown to Thori and his men, the second Takus machine had been moved to within 500 feet of the Rhakta trenches.

Revar felt the time was right to send a scouting party to inspect the glacier. The exact area was only 75 feet away but the scouts would need protection. Although Orsov had no idea why Revar wanted to even send a scouting party he agreed to help the group complete their mission safely.

"Fire your laser hand guns at will." Orsov shouted to his warriors. "Let's keep the Rhakta occupied."

All hell broke loose as the Bukai warriors fired a continual stream of laser beams at the Rhakta trench positions. As helpful as this bombardment was, two enemy projectiles still managed to hit the scouting party. The force of which was so violent, it pinned two unfortunate Tardan bodies to the glacier. The four remaining scouts ran on, barely looking back to contemplate the horror they had narrowly escaped. They finally reached the search area that they were instructed to inspect by Revar and found a small indent on the valley glacier wall which gave them some welcome protection.

On the Nardi slope, Lato glanced along the Rhakta trench positions. Everybody looked in readiness. He fired a projectile into the moving Bukai column which was the signal for the simultaneous attack. At this, all of the warriors fired their projectiles instantaneously at the first Takus machine; they flew towards it like a huge swarm of bees. Orsov was thrown back by the force ; it took him a moment to realize that he was still alive. The noise around him became muffled and all he could hear was a high pitched ringing sound. His vision was fuzzy and he fell to the ground, clutching his head in despair. He knew this moment would pass, he had experienced it many times before but it didn't make it any easier.

Almost immediately, a second wave of projectiles roared towards the Takus machine, the mangled wreckage of the front disc forced the projectiles to ricochet in all directions reducing their impact.

As soon as Orsov was able, he ran to check the Takus. The titanium firing disc had taken the full force of the projectiles and was partly destroyed. Miraculously though, the burrowing blades, which had been swept back, remained undamaged, as did the mechanics of the machine. Orsov breathed a sigh of relief, Tak's genius invention was more resilient than he had given credit for.

On the opposite ridge, Wok told the second Takus operator to aim at the Rhakta trench positions .He had no idea the degree of damage that had been caused to Orsov or his machine, regardless, any chance of further attacks had to be eliminated. Within seconds, a hail of laser beams pounded at the high sloped Rhakta positions, the effect was devastating. Rhakta bodies were catapulted skywards amidst the acidic vapour of the blast. The arched ice covering of the Rhakta trenches began to disintegrate too, falling inwards on top of the warriors. The echoing screams of their suffering could be heard all over the Nardi Glacier as the large, heavy snow blocks crushed and suffocated those underneath.

Thori's head dropped in dismay when he saw the effect of Wok's attack. He knew he must retaliate at once but already felt tired.

"Tell the warriors to fire at that damn laser machine." He ordered the warrior leader Urshu who immediately leapt onto his polar bear and rode off behind the trenches shouting Thori's command. Thori then wrote a message for his now devastated left flank, it read;

"Lato you must hold out as long as possible."

He thrust his message between the great talons of his carrier rook. It took off in a blur of flapping wings, veering towards Lato's position. Midway across its flight path, disaster struck as the rook was torn to shreds by laser cross fire. Its large severed head and sheared talons spiralled to the ground making a final, blood splattered etching on the ice below. The killing of the rook now left Lato, Wantu and their remaining warriors completely isolated on the western slopes.

On seeing this, Thori turned and in a gesture of despondency picked up one of his pet rabbits. As he gazed into its huge blue eyes, the rabbit stirred and jumped out of his trembling hands.

"It is a bad sign," Thori muttered to himself. In panic, he screamed " fire the lasers, fire".

On the Bukai's left ridge, Wok nervously stroked his breast plate whilst watching Thori's laser barrage hit the valley wall in front of him. He ordered the Takus operator to fire at the Rhakta trenches. As Wok's lasers hit the trenched targets there was an enormous explosion – as Bukai luck would have it they had achieved a direct hit on the projectile ammunitions store. The force of the explosion launched the projectiles into erratic trajectories miles high. The warriors below ran in every direction in complete panic. The scene was total carnage and the atmosphere was charged with chaos and fear. The falling projectiles cascaded downwards, as they landed they sliced off Rhakta limbs, one of them pierced through the shoulder of Thori, who screamed in pain. Two warriors heard his cry and immediately ran to his aid, Zak followed closely behind. Throi was sitting up with his back propped up against the moist trench wall.

"I am fine" he grumbled dismissing the small crowd that had gathered to see to him. He was clearly struggling to speak but he hadn't taken his mind off the battle. "Is the rocket launcher in position?" he asked.

"Yes," replied Zak

"Then you must take me to it," whispered Thori, "it is our last hope."

"Save your breath Sir" Zak said, recognizing that every word Thori uttered was clearly causing him pain. "Come on, we have to hurry."

The two warriors lifted Thori up and carried him to Zak's saddled polar bear. Thori winced as he was pushed into position on the saddle. Zak sat directly behind him on the bare back of the animal and with a delicate pull of the reins, he guided the polar bear through the billowing smoke from the ammunition explosion. Zak's eyes began to sting. The taste of the smoke made him feel nauseous too. He tried to cover Thori's face with his hand to protect him from the horrible odour and acidity in the air .

CHAPTER 6

SECRETS REVEALED

In the rival camp, Revar was jumping up and down in excitement after hearing the news from the scouting party.

"That's great news my plan can go ahead,"

"So then Revar," smiled Orsov, "do we get to hear your secret plan now?"

"Not quite yet," answered Revar with a sly grin. He turned to the head scout; "Did you check the far side of the glacier wall?"

"We inspected it in great detail sir," replied the senior scout, "we found something very interesting." He paused sensing the importance of his words. Revar and Orsov waited with baited breath. "A 20 foot wide pathway leads up from the far side of the valley wall to a position directly in front of the Nardi Glacer slope."

"Wow, that's perfect." bellowed Revar.

"Perfect for what?" laughed Orsov. Revar looked directly at Orsov's inquisitive face.

"OK," he said proudly, "I will put you out of your misery." Orsov leaned closer, even though Revar wasn't talking any quieter. "When our column reaches the 30 foot wide area of the valley wall, the Takus machine can turn abruptly and start burrowing through it. We should reach the far side very quickly which will enable out troops to move up the slope on the far side of the glacier wall, completely surprising the flank of the Rhakta"

There was a silence.

"Brilliant, absolutely brilliant." exclaimed Orsov, "Why do you always keep the best ideas secret?"

"There is always an element of doubt involving battle plans" said Revar retrospectively, "so I usually make certain of the feasibility aspect first."

Orsov started up the first Takus, setting the huge burrowing blades in motion. He was relieved at the machines resilience after the previous onslaught it had suffered. The razor sharp blades spun around blowing wind into Orsov's face.

On the Nardi glacier slope, the depleted flanks of the Rhakta had reorganised. These small units consisted of only about 750 men each. The bulk of the Rhakta had been wiped out by the enormous fire power of the Bukai.

Thori reached the rocket launcher position at the rear of the trenches. Zak helped him dismount and then called for help. The Rhakta troops were shocked to see their leader so desperately wounded, they rushed to give assistance;

"Has the Bukai laser machine come into view yet?" Thori muttered, unable to see clearly himself through the pain.

"No," replied Zak.

"As soon as it is sighted we must try and destroy it," said Thori as he slumped backwards.

The remainder of the Rhakta regiments were still going strong, they continued to fire upon Wok and Orsov's positions on both sloped valley ridges. Most of the projectiles had little effect though because the Bukai held their shields above their heads as planned. This ploy was proving to be successful. Although, that is not to say they escaped unharmed, some Bukai warriors were seriously injured by stray projectiles that rebounded from the valley ridge and walls.

Orsov reached the valley tunnelling point highlighted by Revar. Within seconds the Takus machine was slicing through the ice barrier. Sure enough it took only moments for the machine to claw and eventually break through the other side of the iced wall on the valley ridge. He led a large column of twelve hundred Bukai though the freezing void.

On the opposite ridge, Wok had witnessed the Revar plan in operation and ordered his Takus 2 operator to do the same.

At the Rhatka trenches Zak was becoming impatient. He could not see the Bukai laser machine advancing up the Bukai's western ridge.

"I wonder how Lato and Wantu are doing at our left flank." Zak pondered, he waited for a reply from Thori but there was silence. He looked behind him to see his leader motionless with his eyes closed. Urshu was next to him holding his hand on his chest.

"He is alive," he assured Zak after seeing the look of horror on his face. "Our leader is just very tired, he is sleeping." Zak lifted an animal skin from their now depleted stores and gently covered Thori. Zak left Thori in the capable and trusting hands of Urshu as he went to find out what was happening to Lato's position. He rode off atop his great while polar bear racing along the glacier at great speed.

"Did you notice the laser machine burrowing a tunnel?" Lato asked Zak as soon as he was in hearing distance.

"No our vision was obscured," replied Zak.

"They are coming" warned Lato. "We have to prepare for hand to hand combat. Our flank will soon be overrun with Bukai warriors." For a fleeting moment, Lato thought he recognized fear flash on Zak's face but it was soon gone.

"Well I must give them credit; they've made a very clever battle manoeuvre. We didn't anticipate it at all. We will prepare nevertheless."

"We will do our best. The battle is not over," agreed Lato

"How close are the Bukai to our trench positions?" Zak asked.

"Very close," replied Lato, "and another column are coming though the opposite valley wall."

"Our great god Kuba will protect you," Zak said sincerely. "I must return to Thori, god Speed." Lato nodded in acknowledgement as Zak snapped on the reins and headed back to his injured leader, praying all the way that he would still be alive upon his return.

"We will need more than the great god Kuba" muttered Lato sadly as Zak's figure slowly receded into the distance.

Lato suddenly heard a loud grinding noise. He knew what it was; the Bukai burrowing machine came into view at the bottom of the sloped left flank. The Bukai warriors were now fanning out behind the machine in a quick and orderly fashion, laser guns at the ready. At the head of the troop carriers and scattered regiments were the standard bearers, holding their flags aloft in a proud display of courage. It was an awesome sight, the mass of shielded Bukai warriors moved forwards up the slope.

Lato, normally so calm began to rush around in a panic, organising his warriors in two lines that formed a right angle. One line faced the advancing Bukai column to their left and the other line faced the Bukai frontal attack.

As the Takus machine moved ever closer, Orsov leapt upon the rear protected area of the machine and with his hands on his hips he bellowed to his troops in a confident manner,

"It is now time for the final assault. If we fight with courage, victory will be ours." As he spoke he spotted Tak and Revar below him and dismounted as the Bukai warriors chanted the Bukai battle cry. "Your brilliant inventiveness must now be matched equally by our collective courage," he said sincerely to his friends.

"My plan got us this far" said Revar arrogantly, "surely we cannot fail now."

"Never underestimate the enemy," snapped Orsov his small eyelids flapping rapidly. "After all they are my fellow Tardan and I know they fight well."

"The Rhakta must realise" Tak interjected, "that they are hopelessly outnumbered, if we surround them they have no choice but to relent."

"Yes, maybe" said Orsov thoughtfully, "if we can link up with Wok's column on the opposite flank then battle victory may indeed be ours. Still, let's not be complacent" he added as a warning.

Orsov ordered Tak and Revar to take control of the Bukai hoardes. They took their position just behind the front row of the shielded warriors.

The swirling gaseous stream from the Takus was making Orsov feel nauseous, he knelt down holding his brow. The stench took control of his senses for a moment but he was soon back on his feet.

Wok's Takus had now successfully burrowed through the other glacier wall and his troops were marching towards the other Rhakta flank. He was firing indiscriminately at the areas of Rhakta resistance. Being a great organiser, Wok had set out his column of warriors as three large units. The main unit was positioned directly behind his Takus machine; his other two units were 150 meters apart, on either side of the Takus burrowing machine.

"Give me your flag," Wok shouted to one of the standard bearers. Wok climbed on to the rear elevated platform of the moving Takus. His shining armour reflected the snake insignia of the fluttering flag as he stood in a defiant posture .

"When we get near the trench positions" he commanded, "spread out and merge with our two other units, together we can swamp the trench positions of the Rhakta."

Suddenly a high pitched sound made Wok turn, he was just in time to see a stream of enemy rockets raging at great speed towards his right hand unit.

Wok looked away in anguish but the awful screams of pain forced his gaze back again. The once perfectly formed Bukai unit was now strewn apart erratically. The charred bodies lay in a twisted heap, like a bizarre puppet grave. Some had even been welded together by the extreme heat of the blast.

CHAPTER 7

WOK FIRES BACK

Wok regained his composure. He ordered the Takus operator to fire a retaliatory barrage of beams in the direction of the centralised Rhakta rocket launcher.

Although the Rhakta rocket strike had been a lethal blow, Zak was still not happy, he had wanted the Takus machine destroyed. Zak assumed that the wayward direction of the rocket strike was obviously the fault of the operator. In angry response Zak climbed the small inside stairway to the operator's seat and aggressively pulled the operator out of his seat.

"Go and guard Thori," he snapped "Maybe you can do that simple task!" The operator bundled down the spiral stairs and scuffled along to his leaders' battle position. Zak's fingers pushed the computerized buttons. The large disc holding the rocket launchers spun around, simultaneously accompanied by a loud grinding sound which caused a fleeting look of alarm on Zak's hairy features. He didn't stop though, Zak was blind with determination; he continued the sequence despite the faint blue line of smoke that rose from the controls and the pungent burning smell that overcame his nostrils.

The Rhakta launcher abruptly stopped revolving when in place. Zak pushed the attack button without a moment's thought. The whole machine reared up as the rockets were ejected in unison. The rockets sped in the direction of the Bukai ambush and the explosion that followed was immense. Zak breathed a sigh of relief, partly because the rocket launcher hadn't blown up on its self.

His relief was short lived though, his heart dropped when he saw the ghostly figure of the Takus machine emerge through the smoke of the blast, still undamaged. The rockets had impacted 10 meters to the right of its intended target; blowing apart three Bukai troop carrying trailers instead. This unnerved Zak as he frantically tried to re-set the launch computer for another strike.

Wok felt anger build up inside him as he witnessed his Bukai faction get torn apart by the Rhakta rockets but he was even more anxious that the next strike might destroy his much loved Takus machine.

"That's two blasts from the Rhakta launcher and you still haven't struck back. Attack now Fire! Fire! Fire!" he screamed at his tribe, spitting and waving his short hairy arms.

The complicated laser sequence of the Takus machine was locked on to Zak's position; the lasers hit their target with the speed and resemblance of a torch beam. Zak saw it coming and started to run, as it hit he was sent spinning and landed in a crumpled heap 30 meters away. The metal from the now exploded launcher ploughed into the defending Rhakta troops severing limbs with the ease of a knife through butter.

Zarov The bird trainer ran to Zak's aid. He lay there blood oozing through the lacerations in his protective leather. With a look of concern Zarov glanced down, "Zak, we must move you to a safe position," he said kindly.

Another warrior arrived and together they pulled Zak towards a small ridge of ice. No words were spoken as they dragged him away, leaving a blood covered trail behind them. When they finally reached the ridge the warrior asked Zarov if he thought Zak would pull through.

"I don't know," admitted Zarov, "but he seems alright for now. Stay with him, I need to get back to the battle."

Zaks's eyes suddenly flickered before opening wide with pained determination. "We still have another bird at our disposal. Send a despatch to Lato." Zarov shook his head back and forth with a despondent look.

"The bird is dead" Zarov whispered. "Lato will have to use his own initiative now." Zarov saw the look of hope drain from his comrade's face as he left to help Thori.

Thori had been well protected when the rocket launcher was attacked which was surprising considering his proximity to it. He had been lying under the elevated rear of the launch pad. Zarov carried him to the relative safety of the smouldering trenches where he was tended to as best as possible.

The battle was now entering a crucial stage with the two flanks of the Rhakta besieged by the relentless Bukai warriors. The Rhatkta were not giving in though, they had reorganised again and were firing from their trench positions but the projectiles had little or no effect on the sophisticated Bukai body defence shields.

Wok who had been amazed at the power of his Takus laser strikes spotted Orsov's troops and ordered his units to encircle the Rhakta trench positions to try and link up. Wok's left hand unit immediately moved around to the rear of the Rhakta trenches . On the other flank Orsov and his troops did the same.

Orsov's damaged machine rumbled to a halt next to Wok. They ran towards each other and embraced.

"It is almost over now my loyal friend." Wok said gently as he pushed Orsov away from him and smiled proudly.

"Almost," said Orsov, who was always cautious. "We must wait for the two front columns to fully merge and only then can we properly close the net."

They took cover behind the Takus machines. In this protected position the conversation continued,

"Surely we won't need to kill them all," said Orsov, scratching his long ears nervously. He hated these tribal fights, it always felt so wrong to kill any Tardan's, even the Rhakta.

"No definitely not," agreed Wok, to Orsov's relief. "I see this as the perfect time to try and work out a lasting peace formula between our people. We cannot go on fighting forever."

"Seriously?" shouted a familiar voice behind them. The pair turned to see Revar, standing tall leering over them with a look of disgust on his face. "We must destroy them all and this is a perfect opportunity to wipe them out. We will be victorious for generations to come."

Wok and Orsov looked at each other with mutual understanding. Wok reached up and grasped Revar's blood splattered arm, which seemed to be a symbol for the blood loss of the day. He understood that many Bukai had died during the battle and he could see that Revar didn't want those deaths to stop.

"You must understand," he said calmly looking up at Revar, "if we can achieve a peace settlement now then we can look forward to the future but if we wipe out the men here today, we still don't kill the tribe itself. They will eventually be back. "

Revar shook his head angrily it was clear his thoughts were turning to total genocide. Wok knew he needed to enforce his authority.

"Your solution may be acceptable in Noron culture," he snapped "but my ideas are very different and I am in charge. Don't forget that I am looking for a peace deal with us on the winning side; I am not sacrificing our superiority." Revar looked down into Woks face with unfeeling eyes and sharply turned away.

Wok climbed up on to the Takus machine. He timed it perfectly as he could see the two valley ridge columns of warriors complete the encirclement of the Rhakta.

"At my command" he shouted to his tribe, "we will close the circle. Now listen to my words carefully; do not kill the entire enemy. Stop firing the instant you see their surrender flag. Today we will show compassion in our victory." He ordered the disgruntled Revar to take one of the captured polar bears and spread the message to the rest of the troops. He knew Revar would hate this, it was like rubbing salt into the wound, but he smiled to himself relishing the power of his authority.

At the Rhakta's left hand trenches, Lato and Wantu had now resigned themselves to the fact that hand to hand combat was inevitable. They knew the Bukai far outnumbered them and their chances were slim.

"We must make an important decision," said Wantu to Lato. "Do we fight till the death or surrender?"

"We take instruction from our great leader Thori," said Lato, secretly glad not to have to make this decision himself. "We will only stop if we see the surrender flag waved at Thori's position. Our warriors must arm themselves with their ancient curved sabres, for the projectiles take too long to reload at close quarters."

Orsov's segment of the closing circle of warriors was now almost upon Lato's position.

"Out of the trenches,' Lato commanded his warriors. "It is now or never, we must break through their lines." Almost as soon as he spoke a Bukai laser beam pierced the trench wall behind him, splitting the ice into fragments and instantaneously melting it in a plume of steam.

"Out of the trenches now move!" He repeated more urgently than before. The Rhakta warriors moved on spurred by adrenalin. As soon as they broke through the Bukai forward position, a hail of Bukai laser beams tore into the Rhakta's defiant defences but still they moved forward courageously, stumbling over the dead bodies of their comrades. With sabres and lasers held high, the opposing armies collided in a metallic chaos of clashing steel.

During the fighting Lato came face to face with Orsov. They hesitated for a split second and as they stared at each other, it was as if they were oblivious to the fierce clashes all around them. Coming to his senses quickly Lato lunged down with his sabre and slit through the shoulder joint of Orsov's armour protection, piercing deep into his flesh. Orsov fell back moaning. Lato lifted his sabre above his head with both hands, he was about to bring it down on Orsov's head when he was bundled backwards making him drop his blade. Orsov looked up and saw Eli his fellow Bukai warrior standing above him, he had never been more grateful to see him.

Lato went to grab his sabre and finish the job. He felt as if he had been robbed of a significant kill. He knew that Orsov was a high ranking commander of the opposition, as was his saviour, Eli. He would make them both pay. But Lato didn't get a chance, the Rhakta were being mercilessly pushed back by the overwhelming force of the Bukai numbers and before he could gather his senses, his weapon and locate Orsov he was forced into hand to hand combat with other lower ranking Bukai warriors, he had to fight for his life.

Meanwhile on the opposite slope, Thori had been told of the grave situation. He knew it was only a matter of time before the full circle of enclosing Bukai warriors reached them also.

Thori beckoned Urshu with a weak wave of his arm and Urshu responded,

"It is hopeless," Thori admitted, "we must surrender. I must save my people from needless slaughter."

"No sir," protested Urshu, "We should fight on, we must fight on until the last Rhakta falls. It is our honour at stake here which is more important than our lives."

"No it is not," said Thori, equally as passionate as Urshu. "We must save our nation." Thori tried to keep speaking but his head slumped forward. He was weak from the earlier attack and could no longer fight the tiredness that overcame him. Urshu laid him back gently and pondered what his leader had said. He contemplated ignoring Thori's instructions; he believed in his heart that Thori was wrong and that the Rhakta should keep fighting. He quickly shook off the thought, despite his own personal opinion, Thori was his leader and he must obey his instructions. He sent the word to the troops to surrender and the word spread quickly. White flags appeared, dotted throughout the trenches. The Rhakta had officially surrendered.

The scene all around Wok was amazing, the huge circle of warriors were dancing in jubilation, and helmets were thrown aloft as the excitement reached a crescendo. To catch the attention of his ecstatic warriors, Wok fired a laser signal skywards. When the celebrations had diminished a little the only sound to be heard was splintering ice. The heat emitted from the previous laser attacks was now causing plumes of steam to rise and sweep into the faces of the attentive warriors. They stood there anxious to hear the words of their leader. From his position on top of the rear elevated platform of the Takus 2 machine, he spoke to the Tardan nation.

"It is over" he said triumphantly. "From this day forward we shall work together with the Rhakta to build one nation. It is the only way to end the strife. We must bury our differences along with our dead and make sure battles like this one never occur again. Now go and tend to the wounded." The warriors dispersed, stunned by the words of their leader.

CHAPTER 8

THE AFTERMATH OF WAR

As Wok descended from his position he saw Tak.

"How is Orsov?" he asked concerned. "Will he live?

"Yes, I believe he will be fine." Tak replied reassuringly.

Wok breathed an audible sigh of relief and instructed Tak to take him to Orsov's side.

Orsov was lying in the trench; he held his shoulder tightly, grimacing in pain. Despite this, he wore a faint smile upon his face.

"I thought you were dead," laughed Wok.

"Me? Never!" retorted Orsov. "It is too easy to die, I always choose the more difficult path."

"It does look quite bad," said Wok bluntly "that arm may even need to be amputated." Orsov tried to keep a calm appearance although the thought of losing an arm seemed as frightening as death itself. He didn't hide it well enough though and Wok saw the fear in his eyes.

"Don't worry," said Wok reassuringly. "Wasul, our doctor of herbs and potions will work wonders with you I am sure."

"I hope so," muttered Orsov.

"I must go and see Thori to extend my hand of peace officially," said Wok. Orsov smiled. He could not believe the change he had seen in his leader recently. Wok had always been a Tardan in respect and honour, but the compassion understanding and empathy he had shown in the last couple of days was something entirely new. He watched Wok mount and ride off on the tusked polar bear as he wondered what had brought it on and indeed if it would last.

The remainder of Thori's battle leaders and warriors were gathered together amidst the smouldering wreckage of their once powerful rocket launchers. Thori had regained consciousness; his eyes scoured the expressions of gloom in his warrior's faces.

"Thori, look" instructed Lato gloomily. "The Bukai leaders are approaching."

"We must hold our heads high, we are not disgraced," muttered Thori. Unfortunately, his words fell upon deaf ears.

As they rode forward, Wok and Tak were joined by Revar and Eli. Together the four strong Bukai delegation trotted towards the Rhakta warlords, passing scenes of destruction and death which made even these battle hardened warriors shudder in horror.

Rhakta heads were hung low when the Bukai delegation finally arrived. Wok shouted at his men.

"Form a line facing the Rhakta leaders, but remain mounted. We will arrange a peace treaty to be signed at a later date." The huge tusked polar bears were rearing up and down almost sensing the importance of the situation.

Wok came face to face with Thori and looked down upon him. Thori had no idea how his rival would react to victory but knew his fate and that of his people was no longer in his own hands.

"Your troops fought a heroic battle," Wok acknowledged, "It is a pity there has to be a loser. Let us hope the future will be kinder to both our factions." Thori's head rose with a painful expression.

"The loss of many lives makes me feel sick inside," said Thori in a voice so full of anguish it was barely audible from Wok's high position. Lato repeated his leader's words for clarification. "It will always be a horrible reminder to me of the futility of war." Thori continued. "If you are to be gracious enough to want a future of peace then we must fully accept and appreciate your humility. We must ensure our people live in harmony. Let us put our resources together and protect each other once again."

Wok had expected a more hostile response; he remained silent for a few seconds appreciating the amazing fact that both Tardan leaders appeared to be on the same train of thought for once. He leaned forward and brushed the long white hair of his polar bear's head.

"Those are wise words Thori, we shall build our future upon them." He said. "In fourteen lunar orbits we shall meet again and put our thoughts into writing. You and your leaders must come to my underground domain to countersign this historical pact."

Thori looked at Wok and nodded his head in agreement. Wok then shouted to everyone present;

"It is done – in fourteen lunar orbits we will meet and make history. Now we will bury and grieve for our dead."

He tugged on the reins of his polar bear, it then reared up on to both hind legs and let out a shrieking roar. As it came gradually down onto all fours again Wok pointed its head in the direction of his own warriors and clicked his heels. The bear sped off, followed by Revar, Eli and Tak.

As the Bukai quartet moved off through the murky war polluted surroundings into the distance Thori summoned his leaders gesturing weakly with his arm.

"Is Zak alright?" he whispered painfully.

"Yes he is feeling a lot better now," said Lato

"Good," said Thori. "We will now return to our homes and start anew. Pick up the wounded and put the dead in our trenches."

"Should they not be buried at our ancient holy grounds?" questioned Zarov.

"No they will be left here as a further reminder of this terrible day," Replied Thori in a stern voice. At this, the dejected Rhakta warriors began to disperse and carry out their leaders order.

Within a short time, the Thori command had been completed and the Rhakta were heading home, using the same route that they had marched on with great fervour and confidence the day before.

In contrast the jubilant Bukai celebrated continuously on the journey home, Revars name was being chanted incessantly. It was obvious that the great battle manoeuvre with the Takus burrowing machine had won over the hearts and minds of the warriors.

Orsov and Revar walked side by side back through the burrowed ice cave, "so when did you create this battle plan?" Orsov enquired, "did you just make it up as you went along?" he laughed.

"No" said Revar abruptly, not enjoying his intelligence being mocked, even if it was in jest, "the missing link was the great secret burial grounds of the Rhakta and also how both the Bukai and Rhakta worship the same god Kuba."

"Sorry, you have lost me" said Orsov, "I don't understand"

"You will" teased Revar, "but not until the treaty meeting"

"Typical just typical" laughed Orsov.

Chapter 9

UNION

The rich sweet aroma from Wok's carefully cultivated vineyards made Thori's nostrils twitch. It was a fresh but unfamiliar smell that he could definitely learn to appreciate. As he glanced around Wok's huge underground city, his thoughts filled with the battle that had brought him here. He wanted to work for a better future for the Tardan people but that didn't take away the overwhelming feeling of defeat.

Thori had brought many of his Rhakta tribe members along with him including all of his trusted leaders. The Rhakta and Bukai now mingled together for the first time in living memory. It struck Thori how physically similar everyone was, the lines of division were clearly Tardan made and not natural. Sadly however, he also noted that he could easily pick out his warriors by their defeatist stance in comparison with the jubilant Bukai warriors. They may have come to this underground cavern as equals but no-one had forgotten who the winners and the losers were.

A sudden roar from the Bukai hoards brought Thori's troubled thoughts back to stark reality. He looked in the direction of all the noise, nervously running his fingers through the fine hair of his bearskin wrap. In the crowd he could see a proud face emerging – it was Wok.

He was resplendent in a white leather all in one outfit; he certainly knew how to dress for the occasion. Thori and his closest advisers were waiting on the elevated stage, positioned at the treaty table which was situated at the far end of a huge tiered arena. It seemed an eternity before Wok finally arrived to meet them; he made his way down slowly waving and working the crowd like a boxer preparing for a fight. He was followed by his own closest leaders. He thrust his fist in the air repeatedly as his warriors mirrored his actions and cheered.

"Do you have to" Thori whispered into his ear as they embraced at the front of the stage. "We are supposed to be here as equals, you are rubbing salt in the wounds. This is a peace treaty there should be no winner. Maybe your previous words are already just folklore?"

Wok pulled away from the embrace and looked into Thori's defeated eyes. He could see that Thori's attitude was rooted in the loss of the last battle and concluded that there was nothing wrong with his own behaviour. Wok and Thori both stared at each other for a few seconds both expressions were stern, the crowd had silenced as everyone watched and wondered what would happen. The atmosphere was tense.

Suddenly Wok's expression broke into a smile and he held his arms in an open gesture to Thori. "Come, come now Thori" he said with a light hint of arrogance that only Thori could sense. "Surely you don't think I would revel in your misfortune? Come let's stand together. Let's show our people that we are united." The crowd still held their breath in a deathly hush. Wok clasped Thori's hand to his and raised their two arms together. "The meeting will commence!" He announced. "Speak up if you have a suggestion or question. This will be a constructive meeting everyone will have their say."

Wok gestured to the commanders on both tribes to come to the front and address the Tardan and Bukai masses. Orsov, Eli, Zak, Revar, Lato, Wantu, Urshu and Tak all stood proudly and bowed as they were met with a deafening roar of appreciation. Thori and Wok edged towards the treaty table and were followed by their loyal men.

Thori suddenly stumbled, grasping his injured shoulder.

"It is beginning to hurt again." He whispered to Wok.

"I had almost forgotten about your injury," said Wok with a look of sincere concern. "You have made a remarkable recovery I will summon Wasul. He will give you a pain killer"

"No, I will be alright," Thori grimaced trying to hide the pain.

"Let me do something for you, please. I want to help you," Wok said. "Take a look at Orsov; Wasul has worked wonders with him"

Thori paused for a moment and shrugged his small rounded shoulders. "Ok," he finally said. "In the spirit of today I will accept your assistance," although he wasn't sure if he would have done the same if the pain hadn't been so severe.

"Good! That is sorted" Bellowed Wok as he instructed one of his warriors to bring Wasul to the table.

They all took their seats, with Thori and Wok sitting at opposite ends and their commanders intermingled on the other seats. Orsov banged his fist on the heavy, oak table to get everyone's attention.

"I have a small surprise for our visitors" he announced. Bending sideways he dragged a casket from under the table and prised it open. "Surely an occasion like this deserves to be honoured by moistening the palate." His hands reached underneath the velvet draped coverings of the casket. He stood up as he produced a magnificent golden tray full of long stemmed jewel encrusted gold goblets. Everyone marvelled at their exquisite beauty.

"Now the good part" said Orsov in his usual chirpy manner. He lifted a goblet and dipped it straight into the jug of red wine. When the goblet had been filled he handed it straight to Thori whose small hairy hand became moist from the dripping cup. Orsov continued to fill the other cups so that everyone at the treaty table had a drink.

"Our great ancestors have passed these goblets down through the ages," said Wok. "I have kept them hidden until now because I did not think any occasion could merit their use but today is different. I am glad that you and your people are here to share it with me." Wok held his cup up towards Thori and Thori mirrored his gesture. As he put the goblet back down his eyes were drawn to the stunning colour mixture of the deep red wine and the gold goblet.

Suddenly, Thori felt a soothing feeling run over his shoulder, he immediately assumed the wine must have been very strong. "How do you feel?" asked Wasul. Thori jumped, realising the Bukai potion doctor was the one supplying the pain relief and was doing so with just a simple touch.

"The pain is easing!" Thori replied in amazement. "You seem to have potions oozing from your hands." The hair on Wasul's face was long and it was swept back and upwards, coming to twin peaks above his deep set blue eyes. Even his stare seemed to have a hypnotic power. "I feel incredible warmth coming over my shoulder. You have the gift of healing with your body and mind."

"Not always" said Wasul modestly. "Sometimes it does not work; it is then that I use my potions. My powers depend on the recipient. Your mind is clearly receptive."

"I can see by your expression, Thori that the pain has stopped." Wok interrupted from the other end of the table.

"It sure has," smiled Thori "Can I keep Wasul as a personal aid?"

"Now behave your self Thori," laughed wok. "Don't start our union by stealing my people."

The smiles couldn't hide the tension.

CHAPTER 10

TENSE DECISIONS

Over the course of the day, the atmosphere appeared to be softening. The Tardan's mixed and mingled, drank and digressed. Wok stood up suddenly interrupting the mood; "Now the serious business of the treaty signing, my personal aid has made out a contract. If you have no objections we will sign it today." Wok passed the contract down the table with each bearer trying to take a quick peek at the contents.

Thori felt tense. He had a quick gulp of wine in hurried anticipation before the document reached him. His fingers browsed through it. His hairy wine soaked face frowned as he studied the paper intently.

The on looking crowd sensed the importance of this moment and were soon awaiting the verdict in respectful silence. Thori felt the pressure on him along with the eyes of hundreds. He started to feel resentful towards Wok; he wished that he could have had more time to study it in greater detail without this strain.

Despite these feelings, Thori was determined not to miss a single line of the treaty. He owed it to his Rhakta tribe. After studying the document carefully several times his expression seemed to change from concentration to frustration. Everyone wondered what was wrong.

"Tell wok to come and see me" Thori whispered to Urshu, "I must query a point on the treaty." Urshu spoke in a low voice to Lato who whispered the message to the person next to him. The message was passed verbally along the line until it reached Wok who sniggered contently.

"No! Tell Thori to come to my end of the table" he announced loud enough for Thori and the rest of the arena to hear.

Thori reluctantly stood up, it was clear Wok planned on keeping the upper hand. He ambled his way towards Wok as the crowd held its breath, not knowing what to expect.

"What about this clause here?" Thori said angrily, his fingernail scraping back and forth on the thick hemp paper. "Respect to be shown to the Bukai faction at all times? In other words, we cannot show dissent or voice strong opinions"

"It doesn't say that" said Wok. "A little bit of respect goes a long way my friend. I meant it with the intent of easing any strain. As soon as the rivalries begin to subside then we can relax the enforced respect as it will become more natural. That is what we both want isn't it?"

Thori thought carefully rubbing his long, slender fingers against the back of Wok's chair. He looked at the faces of his fellow Rhakta warriors mirroring his anguish too. He knew that if he didn't sign there would be more unrest. His struggled, unsure what to do. There was a long silence.

"Alright" he finally said. "But we must change the wording though and enforce respect on both sides. I trust your words Wok but I warn you, if at any time there is the slightest sign of you capitalizing on the situation then I will personally make you sorry."

Wok immediately picked up a quill and changed the wording on the clause;"Respect to be shown to the Bukai and Rhakta factions at all times."

As a symbol of agreement, Thori took the long feather quill from its ink holder and held it up high for the crowd to see. A sweeping wave of excited noise spread across the cavern. After signing their names, the two leaders embraced heartily. Wok's voice echoed around the steamy hot cavern. "It is done" he announced proudly.

All around the table there seemed to be non-stop chatter fuelled by excitement. Eli and Orsov were in particularly good spirits, banging their golden goblets together in a salute to the outcome.

"I thank you once again for saving my life on the battle field Eli" said Orsov gratefully.

"I would do it again in a heartbeat" replied Eli. Orsov leaned in closer to Eli in a gesture of secrecy.

"I have heard rumours," he whispered. "You must tell me, are you having a relationship with the Rhakta girl, Rostia?"

Eli could feel his face heat up, he knew he should lie; he had been lying about his feelings for Rostia for months now and had done so successfully. That may have had something to do with the fact that no one had asked him outright before and certainly not after so much wine had been consumed. His silence now though spoke a million words.

"It's true!" exclaimed Orsov, taking his panicked face as an admission; he was clearly delighted by the news. "I knew it!"

"Please, please don't say anything," begged Eli, his voice quivering with fear. "You know it is forbidden for our tribes to mix."

"You don't need to live in fear any longer," Orsov patted his hairy friend on the shoulder. "Today we made Tardan history – your relationship is a symbol of unity. What better day to announce your love to the world."

"Life just isn't as simple as you would like to believe," Eli's voice remained a whisper. "The war might be over but prejudices will take time to erode."

Orsov's face frowned. "Your right but unless people stand up and show the world that those prejudices are meaningless then they will continue to rule our decisions in life. You have to stand by Rostia, for the sake of Tardan unity." The two friends sat in silence for a moment while the significance of Orsov's words soaked in. "Where is she?" Orsov asked breaking the stillness between them.

Eli pointed his finger to a small Tardan girl with blonde fur covering her gentle features. She was in the front row but unlike those around her who were talking, dancing, laughing and joking, this young Tardan girl stood still and stared at the table, or more specifically at Eli. Without any more thought, Orsov was out of his seat and bounding across the table to the front of the crowd. He held his hand out to Rostia who was clearly alarmed. "Eli wants to speak to you," Orsov announced. Rostia looked around, conscious of who was looking at her.

"Why?" she said trying to look past Orsov at Eli. Surely he hasn't told anyone she thought.

"It will be alright I promise you." Orsov smiled gently at her, he knew she was afraid. She slowly lifted her small hand; he gently held it and pulled her up onto the stage. As they got closer to the table, a gradual silence fell over the whole arena. Eli stood to greet his love, but was awkward and afraid to show any affection. Orsov moved Rostia next to Eli. Everyone watched and wondered what the spectacle was about.

Orsov addressed the entire Tardan gathering. "I present you Eli and Rostia, these two Tardan citizens; one Bukai and one Rhakta, are in love." There was an audible gasp from the cavern. "This ladies and gentlemen is a symbol of what we have achieved today."

"In love" gasped Wok, standing up, "How can this be? Such a relationship has been forbidden until today."

"No" Screamed Thori standing up also, "this will not be allowed."

"Why ever not?" challenged Orsov. "What is the point of us being here today if we are still going to separate Tardan's into tribes. You both just signed a treaty of unity, how can you stand in their way."

"The problem is," snapped Thori " the treaty has only just been signed. These two stand before us as a symbol of law breakers." Eli put his arm around Rostia and she leaned close to him. The secret was out now and they had to face the consequences together.

Eli knew he had to speak out to defend himself; "Orsov is right, today should be about the future not the past but I know we broke the law," he confessed. "I know we are accountable for our actions but love is sometimes stronger than laws. I love this Tardan woman, regardless of the tribe she was born into. She is a kind, caring, strong beautiful and she loves me too." He took a deep breath secretly cursing Orsov for putting him in this position. "So we stand here in front of you all today and await your judgement."

Wok and Thori walked towards each other and met in the middle of the stage to confer in hushed voices.

"Eli is right" Thori said reservedly. 'They have chosen to love each other despite the old laws. We should learn from it."

"I am still angry at their betrayal" said Wok shaking his head. "But I am willing to overlook their criminal behaviour for the sake of unity today"

"Thori and I have agreed," shouted Wok addressing the cavern. "Our Tardan men and women should be free to have relationships with each other regardless of their birth tribes. We accept laws have been broken in the past but in the spirit of the treaty we will allow Eli and Rostia to continue their affair without further challenge."

The cheer from the cavern was deafening. Orsov put his arms around Eli and Rostia, hugging them in uncontained glee. Tears fell down Rostia's cheeks and she wasn't the only one, it was a very emotional moment that was felt by many around the table and within the crowd.

Not everyone was happy though, Lato leered across at Orsov and watched with revulsion as he got so much of the limelight, he wished he had killed him on the battlefield.

Orsov noticed him looking over; with gleeful naivety he approached the Noron. "My friend, you have been very quiet. I must thank you again for your acceptance on the battlefield" Lato nodded his head, disguising his true emotions. There had been no acceptance; Lato thought to himself, Orsov had just been lucky. He felt deep resentment towards his old enemies; he watched as the other Tardan's rejoiced in unity and wondered how a simple piece of paper was supposed to heal generations of rivalry.

As he sat in a daze, Wasul suddenly appeared by his side, "everything alright?" he asked. Lato looked up but his eyes were distant. "What's the matter?" Wasul insisted.

"Nothing, absolutely nothing" replied Lato bitterly. Wasul looked at his old friend with one hairy eyebrow knowingly raised. "Oh, I don't know what is happening to me?" Lato confessed.

"This is a lot to take in, especially after such a great battle. It's all taken its toll on you." said Wasul reassuringly. "You need to rest and you need time to adjust. Concentrate on your work; get stuck in to one of your genius projects. That should help you get back to your old self." Lato lifted his head; he felt a tinge of hope after hearing Wasul's words. Wasul put a reassuring hand on Lato's slender shoulder as he moved off to another part of the arena bundling away on all fours at a swift pace.

Just to the side of Lato, Revar and Wok were arguing in hushed tones. "If it had been your decision we wouldn't be sitting at this table at all?" Wok said in an accusing manner. Revar gazed at his goblet not bothering to even look up at Wok. His smooth fingers ran a path between the sparkling gems on the side of his cup. Wok aggressively pulled on Revar's shoulder. "I am talking to you," he snapped.

"I am sorry," Revar replied, without a hint of sincerity to his voice. "I was just thinking about the battle. We were doing so well but you gave it all up. We could have killed them all and then this wouldn't have been necessary. We had them surrounded – there is no place for mercy in war Wok, you know that. Or at least I thought you did!"

Wok took a deep breath, "This treaty is about the entire Tardan nation. Not Bukai or Rhakta. Your battle plans were impeccable and we could have killed them all but why did we have to? I have a feeling you have more on your mind than this Revar. Please tell me."

"I don't want to discuss it here. I will tell you later when it is quiet and there is no wine to alter our opinions." Wok pondered for a moment, nestling his chin between the index finger and thumb of his right hand.

CHAPTER 11

THE SECRETS OF THE NARDI GLACIER

"What is wrong with you two? Orsov interrupted. "Anyone would have thought we just lost a battle!" Revar shook his head in comical dismay before standing up majestically and addressing the table and the crowd.

"I promised you all that I had some news to share about the Nardi Gracier" he announced confidently.

"At last!" laughed Orsov raising his glass in appreciation. Everyone laughed along and Revar waited for the hi jinks to die down. He began to speak and tell the Tardan nation his secret knowledge. Despite Revar's feelings about how the battle ended, his decision to share his discovery with everyone at the same time was a testament to his acceptance of the treaty and what it stood for. Wok sat back appreciatively listening.

"Millennia ago," he began, "a huge spacecraft landed here in Esterevania. Its exact purpose is unclear but I have found evidence that the occupants of this craft stayed for some time. When the scouts told me about the sloped pathway on the other side of the valley wall I knew for sure my theory was correct."

"What theory?" shouted Zak in his usual impatient tone.

"I knew," continued Revar "that the 30 foot wide slope was indeed a ramp. Wok also confirmed the existence of another ramp on the other side of the valley. These ramps were the guides for huge stabilisers on the spacecraft."

The audience were silent as they tried to comprehend the enormity of Revar's discovery. Everyone had thought they were in the middle of making history, no one had expected a history lesson.

"I ask you all to think about the valley geography." Revar instructed. "Firstly you have a narrow corridor leading to the valley. This is where the enormous atomic fire power needed for the spacecraft take off would be jettisoned. Secondly, you have the two sloped ridges on either side of the valley – a perfect launch pad. It is obvious that the craft must have been enormous. It could not have been simply positioned directly on top of the ridges without causing a collapse. It would have had huge skis positioned under the belly of the craft, resting on the ridges. It would not have taken much to launch it skywards."

The Tardan faces were frowned in concentration as they tried to imagine such a gigantic spacecraft. "Thirdly," Revar was on a roll, "the only thing our two tribes have always agreed about was our ultimate leader and god; Kuba." The Tardan people looked at each other confused. Many wondered why Revar was bringing God into this.

"Kuba was the spacecraft occupant's word for leader. He was their supreme being and was everything to them. This is why the sacred burial grounds of the Rhakta are indeed sacred. This hallowed place was also used by our interstellar visitors as a graveyard which is why Kuba is inscribed on various walls around the grounds." The air was thick with disbelief, but Revar had more to disclose.

"Finally" he said enjoying the absolute attention of so many Tardan's, "I found a written scroll which had been preserved in ice. It took me a while to decipher the strange markings but eventually I did it. It was a take-off sequence for the space craft; it gave precise details of thrust proportions needed, angle of trajectory and such like. At the foot of the scroll was the phrase that read "Long Live Kuba."

Revar stood there in a majestic stance, knowing full well the importance of what he had just said. The only sound that could be heard was the occasional empty magno car sweeping by on the overhead conductors. Everyone in the cavern was waiting anxiously for the leaders to say something but Thori and Wok were also in as much shock as their people.

All of a sudden Wok stood up, all eyes were on him but he could not seem to form words. As soon as he was on his feet he wondered why he was standing in the first place. He ran his fingers up and down the stem of the goblet as he pondered what to say.

"Have you brought the manuscript you found?" he eventually mustered. Revar reached into his long pocket stitched to the outside of his tight fitting hide boots and prised out the important document. He handed it to Wok, whose eyes immediately started to search the hieroglyphics for clues . He could see none. Revar came to his rescue.

"Each symbol has a corresponding meaning. I have printed them on the back of the scroll." Wok scanned the strange language with his mouth open, he marvelled at the ingenuity of Revar.

"Look at this paper, the fabric is in near perfect condition. It is amazing how it has survived all this time." Wok's fingers passed lightly over the relic, pausing to stroke the deep indents of the symbols. He raised it up to his nostrils to see if he could detect any unusual smell but it was odourless. "I am unsure of the ramifications; this puts a whole new meaning into our life now. We have been worshipping someone else's god!" Wok lifted his head and with the voice of a small boy he asked the question, "What should we do?" His eyes were firmly on Thori.

Thori stood also, appreciating the fact that for the first time since his arrival he felt as if he was the Tardan that everyone wanted to listen to. Wok had been so confident and such a show man but this information had completely floored him. Thori was now in a position to take control and he knew it.

Confidently and clearly he addressed the Tardan people; "now we know for certain that it wasn't merely an effigy we worshipped surely that should strengthen our dedication to him. If a race of highly intellectual space travellers worshipped Kuba then who are we to disagree."

His words seemed to resonate with many people. This didn't have to change anything, now they simply had evidence that Kuba was a god to more than just the Tardan people. All of the leaders nodded their heads in appreciative agreement.

Wok looked deep in thought before slowly saying, "I think Thori is right, Kuba is clearly a great god. Are we all in agreement?" he asked those at the treaty table .

"Yes," they all replied. "And you, the Tardan people?" Wok asked directing his attention to the crowd, a massive cheer erupted. The Tardan's shouted, chanted, clapped and stamped their feet. There was an electric charge to the arena as if Kuba himself was there.

As Wok took another sip of wine, Revar reached out and stopped him drinking anymore. Wok looked puzzled. "Is there a problem?" he asked Revar. Without answering Revar poured the remainder of Wok's wine into his own goblet. "I was drinking that!" Wok exclaimed. Revar lifted Woks goblet to eye level and began inspecting the underside of the goblets base. Wok's hairy forehead crinkled with a puzzled expression.

Revar pointed at a strange marking on the bottom of the cup, "Look at this" he said intrigued. "Let me see the manuscript again," his eyes scanned side to side through the symbols. "I don't believe it!" he enthused. "The marking on the goblet matches the symbol of Kuba." Wok stared open mouthed in amazement. "This means that these goblets may have even been used by the supreme leader himself. These markings are the proof."

Wok pushed his goblet away with both hands, almost afraid to touch it. "I should have known a thing of beauty like this cup would only be ..." He paused for a moment before stuttering "fit for a king."

Revar stood to address the Tardan nation, he cleared his throat. "We have a very important announcement for you." The noise in the cavern calmed down. "Finish your drinks, now" he ordered the leaders at the table.

"Why?" asked Orsov puzzled. He was already feeling the effects of the wine to such an extent that drinking half a glass so quickly would not have been the brightest of ideas.

"Do as I say," said Revar with a small wry smile.

"Just finish your drinks" said Wok impatiently. With quizzical looks everybody reluctantly complied.

"Now," continued Revar. "Look at the markings on the base of your goblets?"

Gradually everyone up turned their goblets. All of a sudden there were gasps from the other leaders, hands covered mouths in astonishment.

"Is that the matching symbol for Kuba?" asked Zak.

Revar replied with an even wider smile, "Indeed it is."

"Someone somewhere has meant this to be. It is a sacred sign for us all to heed." Urshu said thoughtfully.

"We now know why our ancestors passed these precious goblets down through the generations?" said Wok. He fell silent, his gaze fixed on the golden masterpiece in front of him. He picked it up placing the goblet in the palm of his hand. As he raised it to face level his eyes scoured every inch of it and admired its intricacy. He kissed the sparkling gems, taking a deep breath as he did so. He shouted, "I think, my friends, it is an appropriate time to close the meeting, take a last look at these wonderful goblets because they will now be taken to a safe place and only used again on very special occasions."

"The imprint of these rare treasures will be in my mind for a long time." Thori announced in a proud commanding voice.

Thori and Wok came to the front of the arena and gripping their hands together they raised them above their heads. Both leaders still held the beautiful goblets in their other hands which they also raised. The crowd went wild with approval. The others at the table stood and clapped along too.

"From now on there will be no Rhakta and Bukai there is only Tardan." said Wok proudly.

"I sincerely hope that we can all work and live together in harmony for it would be such a huge mistake to destroy all the good that has emerged from this meeting," added Thori. The noise of the Tardan's was deafening. As the excitement eventually died down, everyone started to make their way out of the arena.

Orsov took the opportunity to talk to Revar. "Can you take us to the Nardi area tomorrow morning? I want to have a look with a clear head."

"I will take you," agreed Revar, "anything to oblige your inquisitive mind."

Simultaneously, Wok gathered his precious goblets more intent than ever to protect them, he glanced at Tak. "You were not mentioned much during the meeting, but you need to know that your Takus machine remains at the forefront of my mind. Go and celebrate Tak, you are very important to me."

Tak was modest, "I honestly hadn't expected any more praise. I have had enough anyway. Wok nodded in a gesture of appreciation and politely moved towards Thori. "Thori we must thank your people for coming here to make this an historical day."

Orsov's wife Erith, who had been patiently waiting in the crowd, stepped forward to greet him. Her small head rested sideways on Orsov's chest as they both caressed in loving silence. Today had been something Orsov and Erith had dreamt of for years. All they had wanted to do for a long time was to settle down and raise a family without the risk of war hanging over them.

"What did you think?" Orsov asked his wife.

"It went really well from what I could see but it was very noisy in the arena. I could see the most important thing was done." Erith answered.

"Yes that's true," Orsov agreed. "The treaty is signed and we are officially at peace."

Erith and Orsov held each other tightly. More content than ever before. His hand settled on his wife's stomach acknowledging the baby that grew inside her would be born with a brighter future than they had previously expected.

Eli and Rostia arrived at their side. Erith broke away from her husband to embrace Rostia.

"Come my dear," Erith said gently, "It must have been terrible to have been subjected to all that needless carry on." Rostia looked pleased. It was the first time she had really felt at ease with a member of the Bukai tribe.

"Come with us" beckoned Orsov. "We will take you to our home where we can relax and celebrate the future."

The foursome made their way to Orsov's home and passed Wok and Thori shaking hands. "We will be in touch regularly,"they overheard Wok say.

"Of course we will, in fact we must make a point of seeing each other a couple of times during each lunar orbit to discuss any internal problems."

"Go, your people will be wondering where you are."

"My people?" bemused Thori,

"Sorry, I mean our people; it does sound silly after talking so much about unity!"

As Thori walked off, Wok noticed the two couples. "Ah Rostia, I still haven't spoken to you yet have I?" For a moment everything went quiet.

"No" she said, quietly intimidated by the leader of her once rival tribe.

"You know, I got a very nasty fright when Orsov disclosed your relationship. Eli is a trusted friend of mine and I can't pretend I didn't feel somewhat betrayed." The mood was awkward. "But now that it's all out in the open we must get to know each other better. Both of you must come to my residence sometime and we will all have dinner together."

"Is that a promise?" asked Eli smiling, trying to take the tension out of the situation.

"That's a promise." Wok shook hands with each of them and everyone laughed, although it felt slightly forced.

As they continued walking, Erith could not help but notice the structures of each individual house. They were built so differently to her own iced city. "Your homes look much stronger than ours. They are built perfectly, almost as if they are clinging to the cavern walls."

"That's because they have been formed out of the cavern wall itself," said Orsov proudly. "When the city was originally designed we considered building separate houses but we were using explosives in the cavern anyway so it was decided to carve out the dwellings simultaneously. It was quite easy really."

"Our igloo type homes are well built but they are much more open whereas yours have the natural protection of the cavern."

"Well," laughed Orsov, "what do you expect from the superior Tardan tribe." There was a small pause before the rest of the group also laughed.

"You are lucky to be in good company Orsov," Eli spoke in a warning tone. "This new arrangement will take more time for some to get used to than others. There may have been a roaring appreciation today, but don't be mistaken, some Tardan's will not take so easily to the new arrangement. We might find ourselves treading on egg shells for some time. You should think before you speak."

"Oh no, that would be boring." Orsov joked. Despite his appearance, he did understand Eli's warning. He was just clearly too inebriated to take it in right now and obviously extremely lucky to be around Tardan's who shared in his joy of unity and knew how to take a joke.

They crossed over the twenty foot wide road, pushing their way through the high spirited crowd still making their way home from the meeting. After a struggle they finally reached the entrance of Orsov's home. The entrance was about seven feet high and four feet wide with an arced top.

Rostia was stopped in her tracks; she paused to inhale the sweet smell. "Who is growing flowers?" She asked.

"Ah now you are in for a surprise," smiled Orsov as they turned into his home. The foursome had to part the brightly coloured bead strings that hung over the entrance. As they walked in the visitors stood there speechless.

"Oh you're the green fingered ones," Rostia said joyfully as she stared in wonder at the beautiful array of colourful flowers that were all over Orsov and Erith's home. "So which one of you two is on a mission to shame a rainbow?" she asked inquisitively.

"Oh it's not me," admitted Erith. "Orsov has been growing them for months. His obsession started when we found out I was pregnant" She looked at her husband and felt as if she could burst with pride.

"You have a beautiful home," said Eli politely, "although it is different from what I expected." Adding to the colour of the flowers, the walls were adorned with stunning bright paintings; both Eli and Erith noticed that each masterpiece had Orsov's signature at the bottom. Any space on the walls was covered in animal skin; there wasn't a single piece of cavern wall left bare.

"All these years we have known each other and yet it is the first time I have been in your home," Eli said warmly transfixed by one particular picture, "It's the Tuka Mountains" Orsov interrupted his thoughts. "It's the area where the Sheerak body was found."

Suddenly Rostia looked on edge. "What's that noise?" she asked nervously. A heavy groaning sound accompanied echoing footsteps along the hallway.

Erith's loving instinct came to the rescue; she took hold of Rostia's small hand. "It's OK" she said. "It's my Pico helper, don't be alarmed." As she spoke the draped beads were parted by a huge wooden hand and in stepped a seven foot tall figure with piercing red eyes.

"Number 3," Orsov said in a commanding tone. "Perfect timing, please can you go and get another crate of wine from the stores."

"Yes master." The creature replied. No 3 then turned around very slowly. Each metal joint in his wood fibre body creaked as he stumbled through the dangling beads and into the corridor.

Eli noticed Rostia's confused expression, "The Pico are nothing to fear," he assured her. "They were a race of humanoids built by the Noron a long time ago. They live here in our city now along with a small amount of wise old men who are descendants from the ancient Nord forest."

"But what is wrong with his eyes?" she asked Eli tentatively.

"They are very powerful weapons; they can even use their eyes to paralyse their enemy when necessary." Rostia' eyes filled with fear again. "Its ok," Eli continued. "It is only when the Tardan face extreme danger that this function is automatically activated."

"Come," interrupted Orsov "It's been an eventful day, lets relax." He gestured for his guests to sit on the bear skin rugs on the floor, with no seating it was the only option. Rostia was first to sit down on the luscious deep pile. She ran her fingers through the smooth fine fur.

Rostia noticed an overflowing bowl of fruit on the table. After a moment of pondering, she asked, "how did you even get the seeds for these exotic flowers and fruit? Our climate just isn't naturally suitable."

"I got the seeds from a dead Sheerak body," replied Orsov, "the one who was found on the Tuka Mountain. They were in a small pouch tied to his side." The others listened intently. "We have been desperate to learn more about these creatures that we share Esterevania with. The seeds were proof that their climate is very different to our own. We have to give them such care and attention to survive on our side."

"Instead of experimenting with the Sheerak seeds," asked Eli, "why don't we build and experiment with machines that could withstand the Sheerak conditions and then we could visit their land ourselves?"

Orsov agreed nodding his head. "I have spoken to Tak and Revar about this a number of times but they never seem interested."

"Umm," pondered Eli. "Tak has invented the Takus which was a devastating success. Maybe he thinks that he has done enough."

Orsov shrugged, "Maybe, I don't understand it; the Noron mind is usually so inquisitive. Whatever the reason it's up to them now, I'm happy that the Tardan's are at peace. Besides maybe the Sheerak would be hostile if we made it over there?" Erith snuggled in close to Orsov, not liking the idea of any more conflict.

The sound of Number 3 plodding down the corridor again made everybody look towards the doorway. The large Pico figure emerged through the beads carrying a big wooden crate.

"Very good Number 3," said Orsov in a loud and clear tone, "leave it here and you can return to your quarters." Number 3 obediently placed the crate at the corner of the room and turned to leave.

Orsov picked a bottle from the crate, as he pulled the cork the sweet aroma oozed and merged with the oil tainted atmosphere. After taking a sip from the bottle Orsov looked deeply satisfied, "Woks wine, it never loses its taste or texture. It's amazing." He continued to fill the glasses.

Eli offered a word of caution, "We must remember not to overdo things too much tonight. You will have to be up early to visit the Nardi glacier; you know how punctual Revar is."

"One more won't do any harm will it?" Orsov smiled "Let's have one last toast for the treaty" everyone raised their glasses before taking a grateful sip.

After a few short moments Rostia whispered to Eli. "I think it is time we made a move," Eli announced, downing the last of his wine. "Rostia is tired and I would like to show her my home as well."

"It has been a pleasure" smiled Erith warmly. "I hope there will be more visits."

The two couples said their goodbyes; the significance of a simple drink shared between friends was not lost on any of them. It had only been a few short weeks since the last battle and yet so much had changed. It felt as if anything was possible, the future seemed so bright. Quietly, to herself though Rostia wondered, was this all too good to be true?

CHAPTER 12

EXPLORATIONS

The following day, the two couple's met early to give Rostia a tour of the Cavern city. It was hot, sweaty and noisy. The three residents walked with ease and intent, Rostia on the other hand looked dazed as she stared in astonishment at this new world. She had become so close to Eli and yet had never been able to visit his home. She never anticipated just how different his day to day life was to hers.

She became transfixed at the magnocar's that swept by at speed on rails above their heads. "Your transport system is very different to ours. We have a network of ground surface translucent tunnels that our vacuum probes travel through."

"Vacuum probes?" questioned Orsov.

"It works on the de pressurisation theory. In ancient times the pressurised aeroplane was a common means of transport but during flight if the fuselage was damaged there was a rapid decompression. Anyone or anything sitting in the vicinity of the puncture was sucked towards the hole. We have perfected a machine which imitates and controls this de pressurisation function, enabling the probes to travel at great velocity. It's quite a rush," she added.

The other three Tardan's stared at each other, unsure what to say. Rostia's description seemed too complicated and they each struggled to comprehend this strange system.

Rostia hardly noticed their dumb stuck expressions and continued to look in awe at the cavern ceiling. "I can see with such a bustling city why it had to be constructed so high. There would be no room for the Magnocar's on the ground."

"We are used to it," Eli managed to say, "but I can imagine for a stranger it could be quite overwhelming."

From the main perimeter road, Orsov led the way and the tour. They pushed their way through the lively crowds to a huge opaque dome that contained the advanced software used to manufacture the Pico, at the main entrance stood a Pico guard.

"Number 10, meet our new friend Rostia," said Orsov. Introducing her so that the Pico understood that there was no threat from this new face. Erith took Rostia's hand and gently guided her through the entrance. She was more accustomed to the strange creatures now and instead of fearing the unknown as she had last night she was keen to understand their construction.

"Pleased to meet you," said number 10 as its huge wooden fibre hand grasped Rostia's tiny fingers in a surprisingly soft manor. It was obvious to Rostia that it was strong enough to crush her bones to dust and yet it seemed in complete control. The Pico had been living in this city for generations, if there had ever been an issue Rostia would have seen it on the faces of those around her. She felt confident that if Eli and his friends trusted these creatures then so should she.

They all followed Orsov inside the dome. Rostia looked in wonder at the organised piles of spare Pico parts that included hands, feet, legs and arms. She picked up a hand as Eli came up behind her, "Surprised?" he asked.

"Amazed," she corrected. "I just shook hands with one of these. I had never imagined that this technology existed."

"Never underestimate the Noron," said a familiar voice from behind them. They turned to see Revar who shook his humanoid hand with each of them warmly. "Are you ready for our expedition to the Nardi Glacier?"

"Yes definitely," replied Orsov. "Eli and I are looking forward to it."

"Are you two not coming then?" Revar asked the ladies.

"I am very interested in what you have found," Rostia said sincerely, "I am just enjoying the wonders of your fabulous city so much. The difference in your lifestyle and your technology absolutely fascinates me. My own city is just as advanced but you have very distinct technological differences." Once again, the people around Rostia looked puzzled; it was not what any of them were used to hearing from a Tardan.

"I have been studying the blueprints of some of the new machinery and transport we have planned for the future." Revar said changing the subject and the awkward silence. Eli looked at Orsov his mind going back to the previous evening's conversation. Spotting the exchanged glances Revar continued, "I hadn't told you before because I am only now in the final stages, you know I don't like to reveal things too early."

"Are you inventing exploration vehicles for searching the Sheerak land?" Orsov asked excitedly.

"I might be," Revar smiled his usual coy smile that Orsov knew and loved so well.

"Please, tell me more." Rostia's expression was filled with eager curiosity.

"Yes do," interrupted Orsov, "but be sure to use language that Tardan can understand, half the time when you talk to me, my brain just switches off," he teased.

Rostia shook her head disapprovingly, "don't dumb it down for their sake," she said. "I want to understand properly."

"Come on now Rostia," said Eli, "You are Tardan and Revar is Noron, we are a different species with different strengths. We cannot understand the intellect of the Noron or even begin to try."

"Who do you think invented the vacuum probe from my city," Rostia said smugly. Silence fell over the group as they stared open mouthed at this strange Tardan woman. "Yes, it was me," she laughed even though none of them had even found the words to suggest such a thing.

"You have never told me about this before," Eli stuttered, feeling very intimidated by this revelation.

"You never asked dear. To be fair, I can't take all the credit, Wantu and I were partners in its invention." Rostia knew she was unusual in the Tardan community and she didn't know why but her difference had always been celebrated and nurtured in Thori's tribe. As most people knew or at least recognized her and her unique qualities, it had been some time since she had experienced this shocked reaction though and she was definitely enjoying it.

"Come on then Erith," Rostia said smugly. "Let's carry on with this tour shall we." She slipped her arm into Erith's and led her towards the dome exit. "Bye boys," she lifted her arm and waved without even looking back. As they left Erith could be heard stuttering in her offer to take her guest to the leisure centre and the tranquillity base.

Orsov, Revar and Eli followed behind in silence. They were all trying to take in Rostia's revelation and Eli was finding it more difficult than the others. "I just don't understand how we have been together so long and yet I didn't realise how different she was," he pondered. "Not that I mind ..." he quickly added, "it's just ..."

"It's just we have never before met a Tardan like her before." Revar finished his sentence.

"Yes, it is puzzling," agreed Orsov, as they made their way to the Magnocar stop that would take them to the surface.

Within minutes a car pulled up. They stepped in and sat down on the black plush velvet oval seating. As they fastened their seatbelts a row of luminous green lights flashed followed by a purple imprint which spelt ACTIVATED. Immediately there was a jolt and soon they were speeding their way along the magno rail and on their way to explore the Nardi Glacier.

CHAPTER 13

THE SHEERAK CONNECTION

"We are losing altitude Kandor, quick press the vertical thrusters," Kandor immediately followed his captain's instructions and pressed the button frantically.

"It's no use captain. There is no reaction."

"Then try increasing the magnetic field, it may give us more height."

Kandor's scaly three pronged hand moved a succession of small handles upwards. "There is still nothing captain maybe it's the freezing atmosphere."

"It can't be," the captain snapped. "This machine was built to withstand the Tardan climate." Realising that they had little hope of regaining control, the captain knew he had to take steps to prepare for the worst. "Radio our position to the leader."

"This is Kandor to base," his voice was shaking with a mixture of fear and adrenalin. "We are losing altitude. We are almost upon our destination. Send help as soon as possible."

Just as the message was relayed the side of a giant glacier came into view. Kandor started pressing the same ineffective vertical thrusters in desperation.

"The map" the captain exclaimed as he grabbed the priceless brown envelope. The brightness reflecting from the huge glacier lit up the inside of the Sheerak craft, forcing the captain and Kandor to cover their eyes. The spacecraft slammed into the glacier wall.

A few miles to the west, a Tardan scout called Yond was hunting seal. The snow had begun to fall and he was considering making his way back to his underground cavern home despite not having killed anything. His thoughts were interrupted by the sound of a massive explosion echoing through the valley.

He leapt upon his polar bear and rode off in the direction of the blast, as he pounded towards the noise his mind raced as he puzzled over the cause of the explosion. The snow was getting heavier every moment and it was becoming harder to ride in and even more difficult to see. Luckily he knew exactly where he was going; a huge ball of smoke guided him towards the unknown.

Yond reached the explosion area soon after. The thick black smoke wafted into his face, the strong odour wretched his stomach forcing him into a fit of uncontrollable nauseous coughing. As he passed through the smouldering air, his head and stomach eased back to normality. He suddenly spotted a strange looking craft lying on its side; its slick black fuselage was a stark contrast to the heavy white snow. It was in two distinct pieces, the middle of which was a mixture of twisted metal and fire. Yond stared in disbelief, the shape and size of the spacecraft was like nothing he had ever seen before. It was then that he noticed the two bodies lying in the snow.

After dismounting, he descended the glacier slope but in his haste he stumbled and began tumbling down. His careering body came to an abrupt halt as he thumped into one of the lifeless bodies. He lay there with his eyes closed, daring him-self to open them. As he lay there his heart raced with excitement and fear; he opened one eye. The glistening green reptilian skin made him recoil in horror.

"Sheerak!" he bawled. The alien appeared to be a creature of nightmares, its sharp protruding teeth reminded Yond of vampire stories he was told as a child.

He cautiously brushed snow off the body and watched intently for signs of life. His eyes fell upon a brown folder that was lodged firmly in the three pronged hand of the Sheerak creature. It was held tightly on his chest. Yond reached his Tardan hand out and with his eyes squinted in anticipation he lifted two of the lizard fingers up and tried to pull the folder out of the dead Sheerak's grip. He was immediately struck by how strong its fingers were; it took all of his strength to lift just two digits. Finally the folder came loose, with relief Yond let go of the fingers, they snapped shut so quickly that he didn't have the time to move his hand away. The scales on the insides of the fingers were so sharp they sliced through Yond's palm like a hot knife through butter. He shrieked in pain and pulled his hand away. The blood from his wound dripped on to the crisp white snow which had resettled on the body.

Yond knew that he needed to hurry back to the city and see Wasul who would tend to his wound. He gripped his hand tightly trying to stem the blood flow and stood up quickly sending his head into a spin. As he recovered his balance he stopped and stared at the envelope. He pondered for a moment on what was in the envelope. Whatever it was, it must've been important for the Sheerak to have been holding it so tightly in the moment of his death. For a split second he considered opening it but then quickly came back to reality; he knew it wasn't his place to open something so important and decided to take it to his leaders.

Yond clawed his way up the slope to where his bear mount was standing, impassive as ever, before getting on he put the curious brown envelope safely in the saddle satchel. The snow was so heavy that he had to bow his head to protect his face from the freezing temperatures. He occasionally glanced at his computerized compass, its luminous green fascia reassured him he was on the right path.

Despite the challenging conditions, Yond knew that the weather was stabilizing his wound. He couldn't stop thinking about those sharp Sheerak fingers and deadly Sheerak teeth. It was certainly not a creature he wanted to go into hand to hand combat with. He sincerely hoped that they were not on Tardan territory in search of conflict; even with the tribes now working together they had very little chance against those monsters.

Without warning the snow stopped falling as abruptly as it had begun. Glancing up, Yond could see three figures in the distance near the top of the Nardi glacier slope, two Tardan and one Noron. Yond excitedly pulled at the reins and his bear responded with a terrific gallop towards the distant figures. Unfortunately as his speed increased the wound opened up and he started to loose grip. The blood was now spurting through the throbbing wound but still he kept a fixed gaze on the figures at the valley top, determined to make it to them.

Unaware of the drama galloping towards them, Orsov, Revar and Eli were inspecting the area. "It all falls into place now." Eli said nodding, "I can see the two valley ridges are in perfect proportion to each other, the narrow corridor is perfectly in the centre."

"Why did I not think of your theory?" laughed Orsov.

"If you were Noron you may have," retorted Revar. An anguished cry in the distance brought their conversation to a halt. The three friends looked down the slope to see Yond hurtling towards them.

"I think he is hurt," Orsov said frantically. As Yond got closer he completely lost grip and crashed on to the ice below him.

"What happened?" cried Eli as he rushed towards him. Revar was first at his side and immediately cradled Yond's head on his lap.

Yond started ranting; "It's a Sheerak craft! The bodies! So strong! I have the folder!"

"Slow down" pleaded Revar, you're not making any sense." He held Yond's injured hand inspecting it carefully. "How did this happen?" he asked.

"Sheerak fingers are as sharp as blades," screamed Yond through the pain. "His fingers cut me as I took the folder from his dead hands."

"A Sheerak dead body," Orsov exclaimed.

"Yes, on the Tuka mountains," Yond shrieked in frustration. "Their space ship crashed."

"Where is this folder?" Eli asked. Yond reached with his good hand and pointed to the saddle satchel, Eli went over to the bear to retrieve it. Orsov took it out of Eli's hands and started to open it. The long fingernail of Orsov's numbed hand gently slipped under and pushed the flap of the folder up. His heart raced as he withdrew a piece of paper.

"It's a map," he exclaimed. "By the great god Kuba it's a detailed plan of our land". He bent down to show it to Revar and Yond.

Revar gulped in astonishment when he noticed something on the map marked with a cross. "That's the burial ground of Thori." He said shaking his head. "How did they come to possess such information?" For a few moments the four of them were silent. A nervous energy ran between them as their individual minds raced with the consequences of what they had just found.

"First things first," said Eli trying to stay calm. "We must get Yond back to the city for medical attention. We need to consult Wok on our next move anyway."

"And Thori too" corrected Orsov. "You will have to travel with me," he said to Yond. "We will tie your bear behind mine. Revar you should go to Thori and Eli and I will take Yond to Wasul before we find Wok. Bring Thori to our city."

The men immediately jumped into action, working on auto pilot, each of them trying not to contemplate too much. For a short time they had believed in the opportunity of peace, now though, the future was murky once again and that was a more difficult concept for some to accept than others.

CHAPTER 14

SEARCHING SCOUT

The patience of the Sheerak leader finally snapped. He had been trying to keep calm but he couldn't contain his anxiety any longer.

"Go and bring my three commanders back to the palace," he ordered his scout Grapite. "Tell them I fear the worst for Flight Captain One and Kandor." Grapite bowed before his leader who was sitting majestically on his throne of green platinum. The scout knew that Salak could use the radio to contact the various places where his commanders might be but he was too suspicious and paranoid to do so. His leader hadn't always been this way; his distrust of everything and everyone had only developed after the ominous brown envelope had been delivered by Gux. Grapite sometimes wished that the envelope or the map inside didn't exist at all. All it had done was cause trouble, of which there was no end in sight!

Salak searched his gem studded palace hoping for a moments solace. The smoky incense drifted lazily through the air. He studied the shimmering diamond coated shield which had been a gift from his people. His ceremonial spears were inlaid with emerald, topaz, gold and silver; they shone like beacons against the background of scarlet silk. The carved ivory ceiling was embossed with sapphires and ruby's that sparkled like a thousand stars.

Salak's gaze drifted down from the exotic splendour of the ceiling past the rippling silk and finally came to rest upon the contrasting black and yellow leopard skin rug. He nervously prodded the smooth yellow pile with his great webbed toes.

A trickle of sweat fell down his brow to add to his frustrations; "this heat, this incessant heat!" he moaned. He scooped up a tiger skin fan and waved it vigorously in front of his large bulbous head, giving him a cool breeze as he pondered on the safety of Kandor and his captain.

As his leader sat in his ostentatious palace, Grapite was speeding erratically through the Sheerak suburbs in his streamlined dart shaped vehicle. He was on a desperate search for Salak's three commanders. The scout had already searched the known haunts of Salak's superiors but had been unsuccessful; he was beginning to worry that he would never find them.

He glanced down just as he passed over the pyramid shaped School of logicality which had been built for Salak's son Sal who had suffered brain damage after a terrible dart accident; it reminded Grapite that Salak was a fair and good leader. The incident had nearly destroyed Salak; he completely adored his only son and had hoped he would take over as the Sheerak king. Many of Salak's closest advisors had suggested that Sal should be put in an institution, but Salak refused. Instead, he built the innovative school which focused on sensory learning. He allowed other young Sheerak's with disabilities to attend. Some revered Salak for the bold changes he had made but others believed that his actions were a sign of weakness.

Grapite suddenly wondered if he might find what he was looking for at the school and with little other options he pressed his reverse throttle, gliding the craft to a hovering halt. The main vertical thrusts were reduced and landing pads activated. His landing was perfect; the slightest tremor was undetectable as he touched the ground. He descended and ran towards the pyramid door, sliding it open he ran inside, his golden cape fluttering behind him. A strong odour of paint and moulded plastic enveloped him as he scoured the mass of irregular shapes and colours. His mind momentarily got caught in the confusion of it all. The huge plastic and cardboard cubes and spheres were piled up, almost to the pointed roof. The array of colours and brush strokes were erratic and yet dazzling. Some had stripes and spots others had circles, diamonds and stars painted on them.

As he strode forward, he finally caught site of the king's son. Sal was sitting on top of a giant plastic spearhead. He was painting large pink spots on white material. The scout shouted to Sal. "Have you seen the king's commanders? Have they been here today?" Sal bowed his head and stroked his paint splattered cape. He then shrugged his shoulders and responded with his usual blank expression. "Please Sal, this is important" Grapite begged him but to no avail. He realised his efforts were futile and turned away towards the exit; he could hear the shrieking laughter of the deranged Sal echoing through the light filled glass building.

Grapite's mind raced as he wondered where to try next. There was a major crisis unfolding and he couldn't trace the most important Sheerak's. There was only one place left he could think of - the spaceship construction centre. If he couldn't find them there then he was completely out of ideas. The idea of returning to Salak's palace empty handed was not appealing.

It was quicker to run to the centre from the school than to fire up the dart for such a short distance. He headed across the desert to the centre of the city. The main square was tiled in ornate terrazzo. A speaker's podium was situated in the middle of the square which was where the latest news of Salak's government was told to the people. One such bulletin was being read whilst the scout elbowed his way through the attentive audience.

"Our leader Salak has sent an exploratory craft into the Tardan land. We hope that we can further our understanding of these people and advance Sheerak interests across Esterevania"

Wild cheers erupted. Grapite realised that the crowds did not know about the missing craft. He pushed past the crowds and went towards the space centre, he could see three parked darts, emblazoned with the kings tiger emblem and breathed a sigh of relief. The Commanders were here.

The main entrance doors were made of thick dark wood which was broken up by two long panes of stained glass. As the sun shone through the beautiful windows it emitted a radiance equal to the most brilliant of rainbows.

The scout opened the giant doors with the press of a button. Once inside he stood in awe of the sheer size of the building. In the centre of the entrance was an awesome hexagonal shaped dome that towered above him. Large numbers of construction workers were performing various operational tasks on different machines aided by small hovering lifting craft. To his right, he could see a row of large hangers. He hurriedly made his way towards them.

"I am looking for Salak's commanders, do you know where they are?" he asked the engineers.

A tall red suited reptile pointed in the direction of a strange looking craft. "Over there Sir" he said, "they are just putting the final adjustments to the Gyrosphere."

"The what?" queried Grapite,

"The Gyrosphere," repeated the engineer, "it's one of our new inventions, quite ingenious – take a look." Grapite nodded in appreciation before making his way towards the Gyrosphere hanger. As he got near the strange object, he stopped in amazement. Suddenly he saw Golo.

"Oh thank goodness" Grapite exclaimed. "I have been searching all over for you." He became distracted by the machine again, "this new thing of yours – can it fly?"

"Of course it can!" replied Golo, "It looks strange, I know but the manoeuvrability function is good. We named it after the gyroscope. As you can see, there are two gyroscope shaped structures on either side of the main command module and this is what gives it the tremendous slow rotation capability." The scout was transfixed. The reason for this visit had been temporarily blurred by all this technical data. "For velocity of the vertical and horizontal planes we have positioned powerful thrusters all around the craft ..."

Grapite remembered why he was there; he quickly interrupted Golo, "Well It will have to be good." Golo stopped in mid flow, he was slightly affronted to be disturbed in the middle of his boasting about his technical prowess.

"Salak wants you to bring Etar and Nepht to the palace immediately." Grapite continued, ignoring Golo's expression. "I am not at liberty to tell you why but I can assure you it is of extreme importance.

Golo paused for a moment and then bellowed at the top of his voice calling out to Etar and Nepht! "We are needed urgently at the palace. Let's go immediately." His two comrades stepped down from the construction platform surrounding the Gyrospheres and walked to his side.

Without further comment the four of them left the hanger making straight for the exit doorway. Golo radioed traffic control from his parked dart to clear the air space while Grapite ran through the city to retrieve his own dart from the pyramid school.

Grapite caught up with the other three and the four darts flew swiftly in formation. Grapite was delighted to open the air vents as they skimmed over Sala's tropical garden, its perfumed fragrance cleared his head.

CHAPTER 15

MESSAGE FROM GUX

They came to a halt on Salak's elevated turquoise marble landing platform at the rear of the palace. From there they made a hasty departure from the crafts and descended a marble, spiralling stairway which matched the brilliant colour of the platform. When they reached the ornate doorway to the palace the foursome stopped to tidy up their dishevelled red flying suits and golden capes, they held their spherical flight masks underarm.

Golo looked across at his fellow commanders and the well-respected scout, everyone seemed ready. He indicated to the Sheerak doorman that he could inform Salak of their arrival. The doorman hit a huge copper gong with a hammer. The reverberating sound made the scout jump, as it did every time, he could never quite ready himself for this abrupt ritual.

Salak's voice rang out masterfully; "Enter,"

The four marched in, Golo spoke first, "We came as soon as possible Sir." Salak huffed, clearly frustrated with the delay but relieved the wait was finally over. He waved his hand to call over Grapite . He whispered in his ear " speak to Gux and the Burabob crab people and let them know about this situation I really need to know what's going on, bring Gux to me." Grapite then respectfully bowed before making his exit. Secretly he was desperate to know what would be discussed within that room but he knew his place. In many ways he appreciated not being in a position a power, he didn't think he could realistically handle the responsibility and he admired anyone that could.

Salak wasted no time in launching into his announcement, "Not long ago" he began; "I received a distress call from my first flight captain. He was losing altitude and was well inside Tardan territory. We have lost contact with their ship and I am sure he and Kandor have been lost or killed. What is equally distressing is they had the envelope containing the message from Gux." The three leaders looked very nervous. It was indeed a shock to them.

"What caused the crash?" asked Golo. "It can't have been the climate, the specifications were perfect!"

"We don't know," grunted Salak, "but obviously something was wrong or we wouldn't be in this position now." There was an extremely awkward silence in the room. Golo was sure that the ship could have easily handled the harsh climate of the Tardan territory but Salak was clearly not convinced. As Golo had approved the final designs he felt the weight of Salak's disappointment. He knew he could not argue any more.

"What shall we do?" asked Etar, breaking the uncomfortable atmosphere.

"There is only one thing we can do," replied Salak, "We need that document. "I don't want it to fall into Tardan hands." He banged his three pronged hand on the arm of his throne, the anxiety in his voice was audible despite his best efforts to hide it with anger.

"But how can we get there?" asked Nepht, "If the Captains craft has already failed?"

Salak's face contorted in rage, "You three are my best inventors," he shouted, "You have built the Gyrosphere and Dart – both of which you told me were capable of withstanding the deadly Tardan climate."

"Yes Sir" stuttered Etar, "but only in theory and after the crash today ..."

"It is imperative that we find that map" Salak interrupted. "Take two of our darts and seek out the crash site. Their last known position is marked here on this copy of Gux's map." Salak's pronged fingers prodded the paper nervously. Etar picked up the map and put it into his hip pocket.

"Salak, my leader," Golo said gently. "As we make our way to the space centre could you please radio traffic control and inform them that we will be flying imminently. It will save us time when we get there." Salak nodded in agreement, not wanting to mention his irrational fear of the radio being intercepted by the enemy. The three commanders nodded their heads and headed towards the exit.

When they arrived back at the space centre there was an immediate scramble. Two specially fitted Darts were lying in complete readiness for such an event. They had been fitted with an extra strong freeze resistant shroud. The shape of these two darts had been modelled on an original spear which had been made for the king. This spear had been used in many of Salak's hunting expeditions with great success.

The two darts were wheeled into position at the bottom of the steep inclined battle launch pads. At the top of each launch pad, two special dart ejection slide doors had been fitted. Gradually, these stained glass doors opened and allowed the full glare of the sun to pierce through the ever widening gap and into the shaded centre below.

Everything was ready for the imminent launch. Golo, took off first with Nepht and Etar closely following behind. Within moments of their take off suddenly, Golo spotted a stationary passenger dart. He tried frantically to reach his controls and steer clear of it but he was too late. As he collided head on into the Dart his last thoughts were of anger towards his leader who had clearly not contacted traffic control as he had requested. Salak had let him down and he was to pay the ultimate price.

CHAPTER 16

RESPONSIBILITY

He had little time for any other thoughts, as he was soon part of a massive explosion which sent ruptured metal careering in all directions. Luckily, Etar and Nepht were far enough behind Golo that they escaped the blast; they immediately stopped their darts before they became entangled in the carnage, splintered pieces of Golo's craft littered the launch area. The intense light and heat was over powering, they both had to cover their eyes, although this was also partly to avoid watching their friend and colleague get torn to shreds. Both also recognized, as Golo did in his last moments, that this was the fault of Salak.

They exited their darts and slowly walked over towards the carnage. As the smoke cleared, they could see the rear end of the passenger dart, both of their thoughts turned to the passengers and driver who must have been on board. They waded through the smouldering debris covering their faces as best as they could in a brief respite from the burning stench.

"There is nothing we can do here," said Etar shaking his head in disbelief. "The damage has already been done." Nepht felt angry that this accident could have been so easily avoided.

In silence they made their way back to their crafts. Once aboard, Etar radioed on to traffic control. He needed to tell them about the accident and also to make them aware that they would be in the air themselves; a simple task that their leader overlooked. Once airborne the two commanders travelled at a relatively slow speed towards the centre of the city, still shattered by what had happened.

They arrived in the city and parked their darts before heading for the square to talk to the people. Etar took the stand, within moments a crowd of scaly curious Sheerak's had gathered around him. Nepht stood to the side, his head bowed.

"First of all," Etar announced, "I have tragic news," it seemed as if the whole world held its breath. "On our way here there was a terrible accident, Golo collided with a passenger dart and was killed instantly. We are unsure of passenger identities but an investigation will take place. If you have any concerns about lost loved ones then please contact traffic control."

After a few moments the crowds shocked silence was disrupted by confusion. Some voices heckled Etar demanding answers.

"What happened?"

"Why was the passageway not cleared?"

"What was traffic control doing?"

Etar's large lizard arms waved up and down in a calming motion. "I can assure you all," he said in a commanding tone, "there will be a full investigation and who-ever is at fault here will pay the price."

Only Nepht knew the truth and momentarily looked up at Etar to see his face grimacing, Etar was clearly still broken by the event. Nepht on the other hand felt only one emotion; anger. As he stood respectfully by the side of Etar giving the devastating news, his anger raged inside his heart, he felt ready to burst.

"Sadly now is not the time, we have more pressing matters at hand," the crowd whispered to each other wondering what could be more important than the news they had just received.

"We must ready ourselves for an important mission. We are going to the Tardan land. Our mission is to recover the map given to us by Gux the Burabob. It has `been lost after an accident in which we lost two other brave warriors as they explored the enemy area; Kandor and Captain One."

This was almost too much for the crowd to handle, there were audible wails of grief from some of the Sheerak females. Nepht assumed this was from the wife and mother of Kandor who lived just a stone's throw from the square, he was a popular member of the community.

"Now is the time to be strong we must continue our work with even more resolve" said Etar. He turned to a Sheerak he spotted approaching from the hanger. "Are the darts ready for the mission? He asked. The mechanic nodded. "Good, we shall take off without delay. Inform Salak when take-off is complete."

Etar and Nepht were ushered to separate flight preparation rooms. The integral stairways of each dart were open and ready for them to ascend. After a quick salute to each other and the on-looking crowd they boarded the darts. The door closed behind them which left Nepht alone with his devious thoughts.

I will not accept Salak as our leader for another moment. I am the rightful and worthy leader. I will destroy him.

Despite his overwhelming feeling of righteousness he knew that Etar would not allow a coup without a fight. Etar would want Salak to have a fair hearing, something that Nepht had no interest in allowing. Nepht knew that he had to kill Etar.

He pulled on his all in one methane gas pack and helmet and glanced at his full length mirror. The all scarlet flying suit made him wince. He hated the colours that represented Salak; he decided he would have everything scarlet destroyed as a symbol of Salak's death. A small smile played on his vampire grin.

An echoed voice came over the PA system, "clear launch area."

Etar eased himself into his steeply inclined seat. Two aluminium arms thrust out from the fuselage to secure him safely inside. The touch sensors on each arm ensured a secure fastening. He stared through the reinforced reflector windscreen with the mission ahead clear in his mind. He pressed the launch button propelling his dart skywards through the hexagonal dome opening followed closely by Nepht. After hovering briefly in the air, they both sped into the blinding sunlight. Their course was set for the Tuka Mountains.

Back at the palace, Salak was inconsolable for he had just received news of Golo's death.

"It's my fault," He wailed loudly despite being alone. As he wept on his throne a message from the space centre flashed on to his intercom. He glanced over to see that the other launch had been successful; this good news made him feel a little better. He took a deep hot breath, he had to forget the deaths that had already occurred and focus his mind on Etar and Nepht. Their successful mission was his only hope.

Salak suddenly remembered about Gux, as the one initially entrusted with the folder . He hoped Grapite would find Gux safely and that he would be informed of the new developments.

Alone once again Salak could feel the panic and sadness of recent events begin to suffocate him. He used the intercom to call for his pet leopards to be brought to him. As soon as Salak saw the huge beasts bound in and leap towards him he instantly felt calmer. They sat on each side of him purring as his scaly fingers caressed their soft, silky fur. At that very instant, an astral light flare lit up the nearby needle like peaks of the six Esterevanian volcanic mountains . Salak marvelled at the gold coloured jagged structures . He felt even more peace envelop him.

CHAPTER 17

THE HOME OF GUX

Meanwhile, Grapite the secretive Sheerak scout was airborne at high altitude on his mission to find Gux the Burabob crab. He was well clear of the tall peaks and dense green forest, the appearance of which had always reminded him of a giant emerald.

Even though the scout was used to these friendly missions he was overjoyed once again for he loved visiting the nation of the Burabob crab whose existence under the beaches of the Antovian Ocean was simple and tranquil. The pink haze inside his cockpit began to darken as the cool breezes from the ocean activated the heat sensors at the nose of his dart.

A slight touch of turbulence accompanied by the colour change instantly filled him with joy; he knew the journey was almost complete. He set the flight computer for a low sweeping run over the beach; an operational manoeuvre which would announce his arrival to the Burabob.

Coming in at tree top level, the sequence locked onto the vast white sands of the Antovian beach and brought the dart to an abrupt halt. The dart hovered there like a huge red bird waiting effortlessly to swoop at any moment. The scout peered through his cockpit reflector. The beach was stretched out before him like an infinite sandy highway.

Just as he had expected, the arrival of the dart was heard by the Burabob beneath the surface. Excitement began to filter through the dimly lit passageways very quickly. Soon the cavern echoed with a constant pounding sound, hundreds of Burabob pincer arms were beating a merry tune against the bamboo support walls. Baba, one of the Burabob leaders lifted his arm and beat his large skinned drum three times to signal for quiet and order.

"We have clearly heard that our friend Grapite the Sheerak is here, now get plenty of shrimps and prawns ready for him, we know they are his favourite." He headed out to the surface. His tiny phosphorescent eyes flashed in the light of the small wall torches as he made towards the steep exit which led to the beach above. His antennas swayed violently in the strong breeze as he emerged into the open.

Once Baba was outside, more Burabob followed. The scout activated his landing pads after seeing the line of small upright sea creatures waddling towards his craft. The downward blast of his main vertical thruster's blew a mini sand storm as his landing pads sank onto the surface of the beach.

"The smell of the ocean is as invigorating as ever," Grapite shouted over. He strained his voice to be heard as the fierce sea wind nearly knocked him off his feet. There were half a dozen Burabob that had emerged from their hidden domain but more were coming, he could see an ever lengthening line of Burabob all tapping twin bamboo canes together in their customary welcome. When they got closer to the craft they let out a unified squeal to accompany the bamboo rapping like a swarm of chirping crickets.

"Baba, my dear friend, how are you?" said Grapite stooping to stroke the glistening red shell of his Burabob friend.

"I'm fine thank you." He replied. "You know me Grapite, I am always smiling, just like the rest of the Burabob. We are a happy community"

"Have you seen Gux?"

"Not for some time," Baba answered thoughtfully. "He wandered down the beach a while ago . He had a message for the Tardan."

"A message for the Tardan?" Grapite was shocked. "How is he even able to enter the Tardan territory with their harsh climate? We have been forced to build special machines to explore that land. He can't just walk there."

"He wouldn't have walked would he? Baba sniggered. "We, the Burabob crab can swim. He could quite easily cover that distance. It would take a while but it is possible." Grapite didn't bother to question Gux's journey or motives any more, he had other things on his mind now; he could smell something familiar and appealing.

"Baba my friend," he said hopefully, "do you have shrimp?"

"Yes we have some waiting for you in our caverns." He started to walk back to the entrance and beckoned the scout to follow him. The Burabob stopped as they watched Baba and the Sheerak pass them back towards the underground tunnels, they followed on behind.

As they walked, the dark blue waves of the ocean roared and pounded on to the beach, sending a fine spray on to the Sheerak reptile's scales making them glisten and shine like a mirror. To any onlooker, it would have been a comical contrast to see the six foot tall reptile surrounded by crab Burabob's that were knee high next to him.

As Baba stepped on to the top rung of the ladder he paused.

"Remember to take it easy going down the bamboo stairs. After your previous visit we noticed that the steps were working loose." Grapite suddenly felt conscious of his size and clumsiness. He had visited the Burabob many times and become used to their obvious physical differences but knowing he damaged their delicate steps last time made him feel guilty. He carefully descended and made his way along the darkened corridors, he was forced to stoop low because of the lack of head room.

The tunnels were dark. As they continued, the wall torches became more frequent bringing a sudden brightness to the surroundings.

"Nearly there now," reassured Baba even though Grapite knew the distance himself. The damp odour from the shored up surrounding sand gradually gave way to a delicious aroma of sea food. The scout spotted the bamboo archway ahead and breathed a sigh of relief because he knew they were approaching the sleeping quarters of Baba. The archway had been skilfully woven and was covered in pearls.

Once through the archway the low ceilings opened up and Grapite lifted his huge oval head and gently rotated it easing his neck muscles. As he did so he took in his surroundings, the beauty of the Burabob world never ceased to amaze him. It was adorned with a great array of the treasures from the ocean, the centre piece of which was a circular bamboo table covered with sparkling mother of pearl. The four main supports of the table had been formed from huge shells. He was accustomed to seeing decadence, Salaks palace was a sea of jewels and diamonds but he found the natural rustic beauty of the Burabob's home much more appealing.

At the far end of the chamber, the Burabob cook was shrouded in billowing steam coming from his giant boiling pot. The pot was held up by giant clams which had been skilfully fanned out in circular upright fashion and bolted together at the base . The underside of this base had been sealed with papyrus reeds.

"Baba the shrimps are ready." Said the cook. Grapite felt his heart race a little faster with excitement. His fellow Sheerak had no idea how incredible this place was. He was the only one of his species to take the time to meet and greet the Burabob. The rest of the Sheerak nation considered them to be no more than civilised dogs. The scout liked the fact that the truth was his own little treasured secret - as were the shrimps.

Baba waddled over to the coconut shell bowls, picked a big one and scooped it into the pot filling the bowl with shrimps. He passed it to Grapite and then filled a smaller bowl for himself. He smiled as he watched his Sheerak friend eat the shrimps with such obvious appreciation.

He let him finish the bowl before asking him the purpose of his visit.

"As I said earlier," he replied. "I must contact Gux. My leader must speak with him. Unfortunately at the moment Salak is very distressed."

"Why is that?" Baba asked, showing genuine concern.

"Two of our leading pilots have been killed on a mission to the Tardan land." Baba looked concerned. "They were searching an area marked on the map given to us by Gux."

"Gux gave you a map?" questioned Baba, "this is news to me. Wait a moment" Baba interrupted himself. "He did say something about getting instructions from a flying dolphin. The whole thing was so garbled I took no notice. Maybe the two things are connected." He paused, stroking his chin with his pincers. "You know Gux as well as I do," he said regretfully to Grapite. "He is simple minded so we tend not to take him seriously. I wish I had listened to him properly now. It seems as though he is causing trouble all over Esterevania."

"I am sorry I assumed you knew," said Grapite. "Or else I would have come sooner to inform you."

"He left at the last moonrise. He often goes on long journeys so we thought nothing of it," Said Baba. "I am sure he will be back soon."

"Good I hope he returns safely," said the scout.

"I am intrigued as to what this apparent flying dolphin said to him now," wondered Baba

"Well," said Grapite, "apparently Gux has been told a story so fantastic it is hard to believe and yet so detailed it cannot be ignored. I cannot tell you anymore friend. I am sorry but I am under strict instructions from my leader Salak."

The scout then picked at a small piece of bright pink shrimp lodged between his curved serrated teeth.

"Do you believe the story?" Baba asked. The scout looked down and delicately ran his huge pronged claws over the mother of pearl table top.

"I think I do but I am concerned that our forays into the Tardan land will result in conflict." As he spoke there was a commotion at the cavern entrance, both he and Baba stood up to see what it was all about. Two Burabob were helping Gux through the doorway he appeared to be in great pain. Baba went to his side followed by the scout.

"The jeel, the jeel," he screamed in obvious agony.

All the on-looking Burabob became extremely agitated at the mere mention of "the jeel." They beat their small pincers against their shelled bodies.

"The jeel?" questioned Grapite.

Baba turned to face him, his antennae eyes drooped.

"We rarely speak of the jeel, it is a frightening subject for the Burabob," he said sadly. "It is the one natural danger we have to live with. It is a transparent membrane that lives in the sea. It stretches out like a silent deadly blanket. Its enormous proportions sometimes reach the full length of our Antovian beach head. It can draw its unknowing prey deep into its magnetic body with fatal results."

"I was nearly home," Gux cried, "it got me just as I was about to surface. I heard that horrible buzzing sound and rushed out of the water as quick as I could." He shuddered at the memory. "I wasn't quick enough though, it had got hold of my right leg. I fought with all my strength to free myself and eventually I sheared through the membrane using my pincers." He held his leg rocking back and forth.

"You are very lucky," assured Baba stroking his friends shoulder. "We are all lucky; it would have been a sad day to lose you." Baba signalled with his pincers for Grapite to approach. "You have a visitor," he said to Gux.

Grapite was still shocked by the news of the jeel and had momentarily forgotten about the reason for his journey. "How many Burabob have encountered this deadly creature?" He asked. Baba struck the bamboo walls with his pincers clearly uncomfortable with the question.

"Too many," Gux answered.

"Maybe we could help," offered Grapite. "if I see it from altitude I could strike it with lasers."

Baba smiled, it was nice of Grapite to offer but it did strike him as typical of the Sheerak's to want to solve all problems with force. "I doubt it," he replied politely, "it's almost invisible from a distance."

Gux's cries had finally subsided and Baba clearly wanted to change the subject. "Grapite has come to see you Gux." The injured Burabob looked up at the scout intrigued.

Grapite stood taller, remembering his important mission. "Salak wants to see you; I will take you now if you feel fit enough."

Gux nodded and stood up enthusiastically, all be it a little unsteady.

"Take care of Gux. We love him very much." Baba helped the scout to get Gux out of the tunnels. Once on the beach Grapite was able to stretch his tall frame. He could see the pain in the eyes of Gux and instinctively picked him up, cradling him like an infant.

"Can you make it up the stairs?" he asked Gux when they arrived at the dart.

"Yes l will manage," he replied. The scout placed his feet down on the glistening stairway but Gux went straight down onto all fours and plodded up much to the amusement of the scout.

Once they were secure in their seats the scout pressed a rotational retro rocket button. Moments later they were airborne and flying, almost cutting the tops off some trees as they swooped upwards at a steep trajectory.

"Where have you been today then?" Asked the scout

"I've been visiting the Tardan people," he replied openly. Moments passed before the stunned scout could speak.

"Have you actually spoken to them?"

"Yes, I gave them a map as well."

"Are you serious?!" Grapite tried to hide his anger as best as he could. He had thought that the Burabob were on the side of his people not the Tardan's. The idea of those backward people having access to such detailed information about the Sheerak's would not please his leader.

"Of course," Gux replied plainly. "The dolphin gave me two maps; one for the Sheerak and one for the Tardan. I only followed his instructions."

"Why didn't you mention this before?"

"The dolphin said you were to be told only after the delivery of both maps." Gux started to sing to himself as if his revelation meant nothing.

Grapite felt frustrated and anxious. He just wanted to get to Salak quickly, the sooner he knew about the two maps the sooner this burden was off his own shoulders. He pressed the velocity button and the dart surged forward violently throwing them both backwards into their seats. The pair of unlikely travelling companions didn't speak for the remainder of the journey, although Gux continued to sing his little tuneless, incomprehensible song.

As they approached the gleaming Sheerak city, Gux stared in wonder . Mesmerised by the cities brash, bold buildings and lights, he had been here before but the stark difference to his own world always silenced him.

The scout gradually reduced velocity and altitude as they approached the palace. They came to a grinding halt beside Salak's gardens; the sweet scent was overwhelming, even to the Sheerak's. Grapite wondered how the beautiful smell would affect a simple Burabob like Gux who wasn't fortunate enough to smell it so frequently. Gux sat still, appearing to be in an intoxicating daze.

"Come my friend," Grapite urged Gux, "follow me to the palace." They made their way down the elegant steps of the royal residence

The doorman sounded the gong on seeing them approach and they entered together. The scout gently clasped his great claws round the small delicate body of Gux and led him forward to Salak

"At last you are here." Salak wanted to sound majestic but instead he sounded desperate. "Come over here Gux." Salak beckoned. He waddled over as instructed and sat on a small jade flower pot which Salak had upturned for him beside his throne.

"I am hoping you will have some good news to share with us Gux, I can't shake the sadness after the losses we have suffered today."

"From the reaction of Grapite I doubt you will see this news as good", Gux began, leaving Salak shifting uncomfortably in his chair. "There are two maps," he continued. "The second map details your territory, I have given it to the Tardan's"

Salak's reaction was exactly as the scout had expected. He stood and physically recoiled in horror. "This cannot be happening," he exclaimed baring his sharp teeth. Gux instinctively cowered.

"Sir," Grapite interjected, fearful for Gux. "His leader was compassionate but he knew the pressure had been getting to him". Salak turned and glared at his scout, changing the direction of his anger.

Within moments though the red mist lifted, Salak saw the simple Burabob covering his face in fear and his trusted scout anxiously looking on. He slumped back into his chair feeling shaky, ashamed and out of control. There was silence in the palace.

"Why?" he finally asked dejectedly. "What is the reason for the two maps?"

"I honestly don't know," Gux answered nervously. "I just did what the dolphin from Virejus told me to."

"Virejus?" questioned Salak.

"The divine city under the ocean," Gux clarified.

Salak looked to the scout, hoping for some inspiration. They both wondered if they could even believe the story about the dolphin. After all, what could this creature from Virejus gain from sharing these maps? Salak paced up and down picking at some termites lodged in his scales

Salak turned to Grapite, "You might as well know now, when Gux brought the map here there was an inscription written on the back of the chart. I copied it down here"; Salak took a crumpled piece of hemp paper out of his pocket and began to read.

"THIS PAPER IS A TRUE AND AITHENTICATED MAP SHOWING THE WHEREABOUTS OF THE ANCIENT RUINS OF KUBA. THERE ARE UNTOLD RICHES TO BE FOUND WITHIN THIS SACRED PLACE."

"Kuba?" gasped the scout. "But that is a legend handed down from generation to generation. We modern Sheerak's do not believe in such things."

"We must believe it" Salak said passionately. "Imagine if these riches could be ours" Grapite sighed inwardly; he knew his leader was capable of such great goodness but also great greed.

"You need to speak to that dolphin again." Salak ordered Gux.

"I cannot just order a meeting. The dolphin usually summonses me."

The scout shook his head. To him this was further evidence that the dolphin was just a Burabob fantasy.

Salak on the other hand had no doubt that Gux was telling the truth.

Only time would tell who was right.

CHAPTER 18

NEW WAR

Wok sat on the cold floor in his chamber, naked, his stumpy legs were crossed awkwardly. Meditating helped to sooth his uneasy mind. With each breath he lifted his head, filling his lungs through his nose. As he carefully and slowly exhaled, his chin would fall onto his hairy chest.

The sparkling light from Woks surrounding crystal pyramids shone directly onto his serene figure making his eyes flicker at the intensity of the rays. He breathed out mindfully for the last time and stood up looking for his robes. He searched his vast ice palace quickly glancing at the complex patterns created by the array of Walrus tusks embedded into the wall. He shook his head in dismay, he only removed his robe moments before; how could he have forgotten where he put it already?

The benefits of the meditation were already wearing off. He stroked his forehead in frustration. His searching eyes followed the clear, crisp lines of each high backed seal skin chair where he had been sure he had put it. Suddenly he spotted a bright, white material draped over his wine casket at the foot of one of the chairs.

Wok picked up the robe and pulled it over his small hunched shoulders effortlessly. He loved the feeling of the silk next to his rough course hair. He opened his wine casket and took out the ladle floating inside. He slurped impatiently from the overflowing scoop. The strong aroma was reassuring; there may be difficult times ahead but at least his vineyards were still bearing excellent fruit.

A twin fanfare of trumpets brought his musings to a halt. He looked around and saw Orsov who was assisting the injured Yond through the doorway. Wok rushed to their side dropping the ladle in haste.

"What in the name of Kuba has happened?" Wok pulled out a seal skinned chair for Yond to sit on and reached for his injured arm to assist him. Wok's brilliant white robes were now caked in blood. Yond tried to apologise for the mess but Wok wouldn't accept.

"Your priorities are noble my dear Yond," Wok joked, "but your life is more important than a little blood in my chamber. I will summon Wasul."

"We have some news." Orsov interrupted. "Summon all the leaders as well." Wok's face creased in confusion but he could tell by the fearful look on Orsov's face that he didn't have time to question.

Wok ordered his guards to bring the relevant Tardan's not taking his eyes away from Orsov, as if hoping to read his mind. Slowly Tardan's started to arrive. The first of which was Wasul who took over from Orsov and Wok by attending to Yond.

Wok finally looked away from Orsov but he was becoming more visually impatient, his head was aching again as he paced up and down feeling his blood boil with irritation. The atmosphere was tense. Important Tardan community leaders were arriving equally perplexed and asking questions about the meaning of this impromptu meeting to which no one had the answer, well apart from Orsov and Yond and they were staying silent. Unable to take it anymore, Orsov reached into his hip pouch and passed Wok the strange map which Yond had found. Wok opened it apprehensively and then studied it intently. His deep frown said it all.

"Yond found this map on a Sheerak body. He had heard an explosion and went to investigate," Wok didn't look up from the map but Orsov was sure he had seen his hands twitch. "The explosion was the result of a Sheerak spacecraft crashing into a glacier"

Wok continued to stare at the map in silence. He stepped backwards hoping there was still a chair behind him. Luckily there was and he stumbled to a seated position. He held tight to the strange paper as if it were made of gold.

"We have known of the Sheerak's existence," said Orsov,"but now we have proof. They are clearly intelligent and I hate to say, intimidating in the flesh."

Slowly Wok pointed to the X on the map and looked quizzically at Orsov.

"It is near the area where the craft exploded," Orsov answered, understanding Wok's query. "We don't know what it signifies but we will search the area when light is here again." Orsov realised the room was full and deathly silent. All eyes were on him. He spotted Tak and Revar staring open mouthed.

"Maybe," Orsov said so quietly it was hardly audible, "Tak and Revar will now take notice of what I have been telling them." It was a cheap shot and he knew it but he couldn't help himself.

"What have you been telling them?" asked Wok looking between all three of them, watching the humanoids shift uncomfortably.

"I have been trying to encourage them to build more practical spacecraft for exploration of the hotter parts of our world." Orsov said with a bitter tone in his voice. "Revar dismissed me because I am simply Tardan and said he could conjure up a machine at a moment's notice. Well we will see if this is true now wont we."

Revar didn't miss a beat; he stood up immediately giving Wok no opportunity to comment on Orsov's arrogant disclosure. "Great idea, Orsov, You are right I did say that and I will get to work right away." He approached a guard and ordered them to inform the components factory that machine construction would commence immediately. He glanced at Wok to gauge his mood, half expecting to see anger but he was a little concerned to see worry. If Wok doubted him then he doubted himself. Maybe he should have listened to Orsov, even if he did have a simple Tardan mind.

He physically shook his head as a way of dismissing these intrusive thoughts. He continued in his stride, hoping no one saw his personal wobble. "When we went to the Nardi glacier earlier we discussed the superior intelligence of the ancient Kuba followers at length. The size of the spaceship they were able to launch from the valley was enormous;

they must have built it in two halves ready to be joined together when necessary. We have a machine that could be adapted in much the same way, this particular vehicle has been tested to withstand heat during our laser bombardment tests so with some additional tweaks it should be able to cope with the hotter climate of the Sheerak land." Revar felt triumphant at his delivery and couldn't resist slyly smiling at Orsov who avoided his gaze. Of course he knew words meant nothing without substance but he certainly shut Orsov up at this stage.

"But why haven't you told us about these machines before, especially when I've questioned you directly?" snapped Orsov.

Revar shrugged dismissively, "Us humanoids like to think things through fully. Sharing information unnecessarily is a pointless past time."

Wok was clearly anxious and irritated by the whole situation. He too shared Orsov's frustration with Tak and Revar, " they are all supposed to be a community and holding back information feels deceitful". Wok continued "Well, I want to be kept informed on developments with these machines from now on Revar. Sharing this information is no longer pointless." Wok's anger justified Orsov's outburst and once again he felt vindicated. It was now his turn to deliver a sly smile to Revar.

Wok turned his attention to the rest of the room realising that everyone was waiting for him to take leadership. He was now a long way from his earlier meditation. His world had turned upside down since. He gathered himself mentally by taking a deep breath.

"Come everyone and sit" he instructed." He started to arrange the seal skin chairs in a circle and the others followed suit. At this point Thori and his entourage also entered the chamber. Wok didn't think he had ever been so pleased to see the leader of his previous rival tribe. He did not want to handle this pressure alone. The game had suddenly changed, drastically.

"Excellent," exclaimed Wok, greeting his old enemy with open arms. "Now we can start the meeting." keen not to appear as weak as he felt, Wok stood in the centre of the large circle of seated Tardan and spoke in a loud commanding voice;

"First of all I want you all to look at this map," he handed it to Thori first. "Pass it around when you are done." he instructed. "As you will all see, it is a detailed plan of our world but the most important factor is that it has been found on a body of a Sheerak whose spacecraft crash landed in here on the Tukas earlier today."

Although some of the room already knew this information There was still an audible gasp from the chamber. Simultaneously, a strange sweet aroma wafted from Wasul's wonder potion that he had been using on Yond. The moment felt surreal, as if time was standing still.

After some tense moments Wok signalled to Orsov to explain the encounter in more detail. The map was still being passed around the circle. "It was found on a body lying next to a spacecraft which had crashed well inside our territory. It was a very advanced streamlined design, obviously built by the Sheerak who have now proved their intelligence beyond any previous doubt. You will see the map is extremely detailed even the altitudes of the glaciers have been included. It has an X sign, but before anyone asks we don't know the meaning of it as yet. We will explore this at first light."

Zoltan suddenly burst through the main entrance of Woks residence. He was in a complete panic. He scrambled over to where the delegation was seated pushing apart and toppling some chairs in his haste to get to Wok. Zoltan thrust the Gux map into Woks hand. He was too breathless to speak., the entire room looked on puzzled at this dramatic interruption. Wok opened it curiously, initially noticing the writing on the back embossed with an official seal of some sort. He started to read the contents aloud;

"THIS IS A TRUE AND AUTHENTICATED MANUSCRIPT SHOWING THE WHEREABOUTS OF A HIDDEN LAND . IT DESCRIBES THE EXACT LOCATION OF THE ANCIENT CIVILLISIATION OF ESTEREVANIA. IT IS FULL OF TREASURE AND RICHES."

The room was silent and thick with anticipation. Some in the room were distracted from the immediate danger and drawn to the concept of treasure and riches.

"Where did you get this from Zoltan?" Wok asked, finally breaking the silence.

"You wouldn't believe me leader," Zoltan was still out of breath, holding onto his chest as he spoke. He could see by the look on Wok's face that this wasn't enough. He was going to have to share his crazy unbelievable story and just hope that they didn't lock him up for losing his mind. He took a deep breath and began …

"I was fishing when I noticed these strange claw markings, I bent down to have a closer look and while I was looking I heard a peculiar clicking sound behind me I turned around and standing in front of me was a giant crab!" Sniggers could be heard around the room. Zoltan had expected as much but he kept his eyes on Wok, it didn't matter what anyone else thought. He continued. "It was upright and in its right pincer, it was holding this map."

"What on earth did you do?" asked Orsov,

"I just stood there shocked and rooted to the spot. I was sure I was hallucinating. It spoke in a high pitched squeak unlike anything I had heard before, it was going on about a flying dolphin or something, but it definitely told me to give this to Wok. Then he just waddled off towards the sea singing to himself." There was silence, he threw his arms up defensively, "look, I know it sounds ridiculous but this is what happened, I swear!"

"I've heard it all now," mocked Lato. "He is officially crazy." Zolton hated feeling ridiculed; he felt everyone's judging eyes on him and suddenly snapped. He lunged at Lato but was held back by Orsov.

"Calm down everybody," Orsov implored directing it only at Lato and Zoltan. "Wok can I see the map please." Orsov reached to take the map from his leader returning promptly to his spot in-between the sparring pair. After a few moments of studying it he looked up in amazement. "This map here is really detailed. This is the second map like this of our land we have to assume it came from the same source. We cannot discount it lightly."

As if to purposely ease the thick atmosphere Eli interjected, "how tall was the crab?"

Zoltan had calmed a little bit although was still deep breathing from the adrenalin that had coursed through his veins when he wanted to punch Lato. He took a deep breath.

"Almost chest high," he answered, "its shell was bright red in colour just like our own sea food. It had small antennas to house luminous pink eyes. It had small clawed feet at the bottom of its thin legs. I remember thinking that they looked too fragile to support its body weight as it waddled away into the distance."

"Did it say where it came from?" asked Eli,

"No, obviously the ocean but I did think of following it. I decided it was best to get back here as soon as possible, besides it travelled very fast over the ice and was out of sight quickly."

Lato made a disapproving grunt, causing Zoltan to tense again. Orsov, still playing peace maker shifted to ensure he was still standing as a barrier between the pair. "Here", he snapped, thrusting the map towards Lato,"study it for yourself." Lato took it with his bony fingertips looking at it as if it were made of something dirty. Holding it in front of his nose he sniffed.

"Ok," he conceded, "I can smell the ocean."

"Well if you decide to accept it or not Lato," said Wok decisively, "the rest of us need a plan." He rubbed his forehead and gingerly opened one eye staring straight at Revar. "Do you realise we now have to travel into the Sheerak land. Maybe now is the time to tell the rest of the Tardan leadership about your progress."

Revar stood up and opened his arms in his usual confident manner. "I know this is going to be a shock to most of you but we do currently have the capability for such an epic journey." Wok shifted angrily in his seat. He hated being kept in the dark about such important things, it undermined his leadership. "As I said to Orsov before," Revar continued smiling. "It is existing technology we just need to tweak it."

Thori had sat quietly throughout the proceedings thus far, he had not been the leader that the crab had mentioned and this unnerved him. Where ever in the world this crab came from, Thori's name didn't seem relevant. Now though his curiosity got the better of him and he could remain silent no more.

"What type of craft is it?" he asked, before he could get an answer Thori couldn't help himself asking more questions, "Is it easy to handle? Will our pilots be able to learn to fly it safely in a short time? What functions can it perform?"

All these questions didn't put Revar off balance, he continued immediately. "I call it the Pendurotor, it compromises of a basic circular ball and a simple mechanism to propel it. During our tests to develop an outer shell we discovered the extensive elasticity and additional attributes of our newly discovered metal; Laserite. The continual bombardment of lasers upon the new metal did not even mark the material, hence the name Laserite. The machine has great mobility at ground level rotating in conjunction with a main pendulum gear which will be constructed and even transported separately if necessary. The pendulum arm is fitted with a powerful magnet which is positioned at the extremity of the horizontal bar of the main, inverted Tee structure. A small detonation sets the pendulum swinging and as the arm begins to move, the magnet activates motion of the sphere by means of opposite polarity. The polarity of movement function is further helped by the positioning of various magnets on the inner shell of the sphere and the subsequent basic theory of different poles do not attract comes into operation. To control the direction of the Pendurotor the main pendulum can swivel on its primary support. Altitude is achieved by small thrusters positioned all around the outer shell and once airborne they are used to propel back and forward also. But these thrusters have a dual purpose for they are also fitted with lasers for attack and defence and even the spiked ends could be used for attack."

By the time Revar stopped talking the whole room were staring open mouthed in amazement at his intellect and achievement. Tak burst into spontaneous applause and others followed suit. The atmosphere in the chamber had risen and the Tardan territorial love of war was showing again only instead of fighting each other they had a possible common enemy.

Not everyone was excited by this prospect though, Orsov's mind started reeling, "not more fighting I hope not." he said under his breath. "I promised my wife." His thoughts were broken by Wok, clapping his hands together bringing the meeting back to order again.

"First of all Revar," he demanded, "you must go back to the components factory and begin erection of this new phenomenon of yours. You, Thori can stay here until light. Orsov, you and Eli will pick the search party. Yond you can stay until Wasul finishes work on you. Everyone else, this meeting is now closed." Quickly most people dispersed, the atmosphere was tense but charged with possibility, hope and plenty of testosterone.

Revar lingered until most people had left, "Wok," he whispered, "I need to talk to you in private." Wok was concerned. With such an important task ahead he knew the usually focused Revar must have something important on his mind. "Do you remember during the treaty meeting," he asked, "I was going to tell you the reason for wanting to finish off the Rhakta at the battle of the Nardi Glacier." Wok nodded, still feeling confused, "Well my main reason was one of disgust. I was disgusted with myself for not initiating my new machines. We could have won the battle with very little bloodshed. As it was we lost more men than necessary, a lot of whom were good friends. I thought wiping them out would have compensated for my grief" Wok took Revar's white humanoid hand and caressed it between his stark contrasting rough hairy digits.

Wok sighed, he was glad to be able to understand Revar a little better; the humanoids have a completely different skill set and procedures for managing emotions. His strange behaviour that day had certainly left him confused, now however was not the time.

"Revar that is now forgotten," he forced himself to say kindly. "Now is time for action not reflection. We all have moments of weakness, well most do, I myself have to continue to be strong, but I do empathise. Now though you must go and focus on what your good at."

"Thank you my leader" Revar bowed. He vowed to focus on the new united Tardan enemy and promised himself he would never underestimate war again.

At first light Orsov arrived with the search party which consisted of Eli, Lato, Tak and heavily bandaged Yond. Wok stood there clad in a black silk undergarment.

"Yond are you fit?" he asked.

"Yes My wound has closed up rapidly Wasul is a genius."

"Good, now wait here all of you. I just need to quickly change."

"But surely you are not coming?" asked a surprised Orsov .

"Of course, I wouldn't miss this for anything," said Wok excitedly as he shuffled away to get ready for the scouting mission. Wok returned soon after clothed in white seal skin trousers and boots, looking every bit a rock star. "Give the map to Yond he will guide us to the crash site. Let's do this" he said excitedly, "Let's see what awaits us." Everyone followed their leader, each one of them with mixed emotions, even Wok.

CHAPTER 19

FIRST ENCOUNTERS

Etar and Nepht were finally approaching the Tuka Mountains. Nepht guided his dart into the direct firing line behind Etar's craft. He pressed the turbulence seeking laser button and instantly his launch radar moved to a target read position. He felt the power of knowing he could end Etar's life at any time. His scaly finger hovered over the laser button. He visualised the glory of destroying Etar, who was far too loyal to their incompetent leader to be spared.

He could almost feel the heat from the explosion as he imagined his aircraft exploding into a fiery ball. It was a glorious feeling. Nepht took a deep breath and took his finger away from the red button. He needed Etar right now, but his time would come. A sly smile flashed across his face showing his sharp crocodile- like teeth.

"We have cleared the mountains," the doomed voice of Etar interrupted his thoughts over the radio. "We will be approaching the crash site soon."

Both darts began to lower speed and altitude. They scanned the iced terrain for any visible signs of the wreckage; suddenly Nepht noticed his heat sensor receiver was flashing. It had detected body heat.

"Are they alive?" Etar asked excitedly. Nepht was more reserved.

"It's been too long, I doubt it, but something is." They instantaneously spotted 6 small figures.

"Tardan!" Etar announced.

"I see them too" confirmed Nehpt. "Lower your altitude and follow me." The two darts swept over the crash area and made an abrupt 180^0 turn catching the attention of the Tardan below.

Orsov looked up and his gut twisted into a knot. "What in the name of Kuba are they?" he said trying not to be sick.

"I think the Sheerak are looking for their friends," said Yond. A strong sulphur like odour filled the valley as the two crafts headed straight towards the Tardan search party.

This was a momentous moment in the history of Esterevania. The two predominant species, kept apart for generations by climate, were physically in contact for the first time. It was one of those moments where the entire future of the planet seemed to be in the hands of a few. There were some in this group who craved peace and compassion and others who favoured power and war. The question was who was going to win?

"Shall we fire?" Lato asked Wok tentatively. Wok hesitated, inwardly understanding his leadership and responsibilities. He was paralysed by the magnitude of it. If they didn't fire and these Sheerak fired first they stood no chance. On the other hand, what if the Sheerak came with peaceful intentions? What if the Tardan's fired out of fear and sparked a war that was unnecessary. The Tardan's had only just found peace. This was all new ground and no one knew where they stood. At least with the old tribal battles it was clear. Lato's hand moved nervously on the hand laser trigger. The two Sheerak crafts were getting closer.

As they approached Nepht wasn't in any dilemma in fact he didn't delay in pressing the red laser button as soon as the target was locked in position. He would not let those animals even get a chance at damaging a superior Sheerak craft.

He released a deadly laser beam from the hidden undercarriage of his dart. It hit the ice below Eli and Yond, taking the ground literally from beneath their feet. They fell and were instantly crushed to death by the ice that fell in on them. The four other Tardan's were knocked back in different directions by the blast.

"What did you do that for?" Screamed Etar, shocked by the horrific actions of his comrade.

"I had to," snapped Nepht." It was kill or be killed. The weak do not survive." He was irritated that he even had to justify anything.

"You may have just started a war." Etar cried in dismay.

Nepht smiled. That was exactly what he wanted.

On the ground it took a few moments for the smoke and steam to clear. "Everybody all right?" questioned a desperate Orsov. His voice was hoarse and strained from the smoke inhalation.

"No, not all of us are," shouted Wok,

Orsov could suddenly see and his heart sank. The body of his dear friend Eli lay mangled inside a hole, tangled up with the brave Yond . Orsov lost control of his legs and fell to his knees at the edge of the crevice. He didn't have time to grieve though.

"They are coming back," shouted Wok.

Lato had gathered himself and picked up his weapon. The other Tardan's readied themselves.

"Fire!" shouted Wok although his command was not necessary; there was no question any more. All four Tardan men sent laser beams into the sky, hitting the under carriage of the nearest dart.

Unfortunately this was Etar's craft. It exploded instantly into a billion tiny particles that rained down on the Tardan's like a metal winters shower. Etar hadn't even seen it coming, he was gone.

Wok and Tak screamed in delight.

Nepht smiled, he was surprised by the Tardan technology and accuracy. He was even a little worried but he was unreservedly pleased that they had disposed of Etar for him. At least it saved him a job!

His glee didn't last long, he soon realised that the Tardan guns were now aiming their lasers at him. With no time to take aim he immediately pulled up activating the extreme velocity sequence, heading up at a steep 90° angle.

The Tardan's below cheered, more in relief than joy. One more shot from that Sheerak craft and they would have all been toast.

All became quiet on the Tuka Mountains once more; the reality began to set it. They had left with six companions but will only be returning with four.

"What will I tell Rostia?" Orsov sighed. "She loved him so much."

"You will tell her that he died a noble death" said Wok. "He died fighting for his people, for her."
"Fighting" mocked Orsov, "We didn't stand a chance. I am so sick of this, of the death and hatred. I can't do this anymore." He became enraged, he felt the gun in the palm of his hand, it felt as if he was holding a hot stone and allowing it to burn his skin. He threw it as hard as he could and as he did he screamed, a deep gut wrenching scream that soon turned into uncontrollable sobbing. Orsov sat on the snow and cried.

Wok understood this pain but he also knew that this war had just begun; he needed Orsov more than ever. He reached his hand out and pulled him up patting him on the shoulder firmly. "You will," he said kindly, "you will because you love your wife and our people. You will because you believe in our way of life, you will because you are strong. Now come, we must head back home."

Together they silently carried the bodies of their friends and mounted them securely on to their polar bears. Lato quietly pondered about how a body seemed so much heavier after someone had died .

As Wok Lato Orsov and Tak began their walk back they soon spotted Orsov's gun in the snow. "You will need that," said Wok but Orsov just kept on walking.

CHAPTER 20

VIREJUS CALLING

Gux had only just arrived back in his underground home when he felt an impulse to visit the dolphin. He knew that this was a feeling he had to follow. Whenever he listened to his instincts it always led to good things. Without even sitting down he headed straight back out through the bamboo door.

He scurried along the dimly lit tunnels as fast as he could, occasionally looking back to see if he was being followed. After emerging on to the surface he went straight to the ocean, his two small antennae scoured the coastline whilst his back legs waded vigorously up and down, propelling him forward.

Gux knew the route well; he swam straight to the rocky cove where he had met the dolphin many times before. His friend was close by, hovering just above the cave trying to locate the scent of Gux.

Suddenly he caught the familiar waft of the simple and truthful soul of Gux. He looked down to see his small red body already patiently waiting in the cave. Upon meeting, ... the pair enthusiastically greeted each other with a high 5 type action, fin to claw. They both shared a lot of affection for each other and each meeting was full of warmth.

"Why did you call me here" asked Gux innocently. "Have you got another task for me?"

"Not today," smiled the dolphin, in a way only dolphins can, " you have done so well following our instructions Gux, we really appreciate your help. My leader has a plan and it is coming together nicely thanks to you. He wants to show his gratitude. I will take you to him now, you will fly with me."

Gux was overwhelmed, he never considered himself part of anything. He was just doing what his friend had asked him to. He always had a feeling that it was the right thing to do. He couldn't explain it, he didn't need to. He just knew he was following the right path because it felt good. Now, not only was he going to meet this elusive leader but he was actually going to fly with a dolphin!

Before Gux had time to truly digest the concept of flying without a plane, the dolphin had swam underneath him manoeuvring between Gux's legs. Gux instinctively took hold of the fin with his pincers.

"Ready?" asked the dolphin,

"As ready as I'll ever be!" replied Gux laughing to himself at the ridiculous thought of a flying crab (the thought of a flying dolphin didn't seem as ridiculous to him anymore).

"Here we go," said the dolphin as he slowly broke through the surface, gaining speed and momentum as they rose. "Virejus here we come!"

As they pushed through the gentle waves the dolphin's twin membranes spread out and ever so gently they lifted into the air and continued their ascent towards the clouds. They sailed at a steep angle, Gux held on tightly to his friend, he was concerned his pincers might hurt the dolphin but he was too afraid to let go. He rested his head on the back of the dolphin and closed his eyes, too afraid to look anymore.

"You don't mind the cold methane too much?" asked the dolphin.

"No, not at all, it's just the flying part that worries me," squeeked Gux his eyes still shut tight.

Gux could feel the dolphin begin to level out. "You can lift your head now," said the dolphin kindly. "We will not be going any higher and this view is truly breath-taking."

Gradually Gux lifted his small body from the dolphins back and resumed an upright sitting position. The wind made him sway uneasily and he felt nauseous. He was too scared to look down and kept his twin antennae positioned in front of his eyes, blocking his vision.

"What do you think? Isn't it beautiful?" The dolphin had prompted Gux's bravery; he slowly looked down, moving his twin antenna out of the way. The sight that bestowed him nearly forced him to loose balance; he stared in amazement.

From their high altitude he could see the vast white sand of the Antovian beaches. It looked much clearer than he could have ever imagined, he could make out the movement of the ocean and the momentum of the waves as they pounded the shoreline. Gux had flown in a cockpit before but that had left him feeling unconnected, never before in his short life had he ever felt part of the fabric of Esterevania.

"So," the dolphin repeated. "What is your verdict?"

"Amazing," was the only word Gux could muster in a dream like trance.

As the journey continued Gux relaxed into the ride. The dolphin sensed this and became more playful and adventurous; dropping down and rising higher, dancing in the sky and catching the air currents. Gux was delighted and squealed in excitement with each twist and turn. Even at this height Gux could still taste the salt from the ocean. The dense tropical air which carried the salt upwards was lacking in methane and he was forced to take deep breaths.

Gux began to wonder if this journey would ever end. He thought that maybe he would like to spend an eternity up in this exquisite peaceful place.

"Look down" the dolphin suddenly interrupted. "We are heading over there," he pointed his nose to the left and started to descend towards a small coral island. Gux was sure he had passed this part of the ocean before in a plane, how could he have missed it? "Hold on tight," shouted the dolphin, those were three words he didn't need to be told twice. Gux held on for dear life.

The dolphin lowered his left membrane and they began to descend at an exhilarating speed. Gux wasn't sure what was more frightening, going up or down. They didn't appear to be slowing and the island was approaching fast. Even though he trusted his friend, he did panic for a moment that they were about to crash land. Suddenly they levelled off and immediately slowed down, the force of the abrupt change nearly forced Gux off his ride, luckily he was holding on tight.

"Do you notice anything unusual about the island?

Gux looked carefully. "It's formed completely out of multi-coloured coral. It looks as if it's part of a set structure. It doesn't look natural, was it built?"

"That's right Gux you are very observant. We call them location points. We have various areas of this vast ocean to guide us to our hidden city under the waves."

"It seems to be connected underneath?"

"Yes underneath is a coral life line. It stretches all the way to the ocean bed. It enables us to move the location points according to our needs. That's why you have never noticed it before. Only when we intend it to be visible, can you see it."

They glided further on, leaving the coral marker far behind. Gux felt better at this low altitude his breathing was much easier.

"Are we close now?" As he spoke he sensed something above him, before he had time to look he felt something brush against his antennae, he jumped nearly losing his balance. He looked up and was startled to see a huge albatross gliding effortlessly almost on top of them. Its slender white body blotted out the glaring sun.

"There is your answer, we must be nearly there now," said the dolphin. As Gux stared another albatross came into view on the right and another on the left. He looked down to discover one below them. They were surrounded. These flying gracious creatures were so close he could reach out and touch their outstretched wings.

"Get ready for the ocean," Warned the dolphin, he tilted his body down and Gux grabbed his fin firmly. "Now we dive."

Without further warning they plunged into the ocean piercing the surface like a torpedo. Down and down into the deep blue depths they soared until the ocean around them was almost black.

As they went deeper Gux thought he saw a faint luminous light coming from the depths. The sheen became stronger and stronger until he could just about discern a huge green coral dome.

Gux stared in wonderment. "This is your home?"

CHAPTER 21

AN INVITATION

"It's big isn't it," smiled the dolphin, "It is exactly 10 nautical miles in radius." The green light emitting from the coral city brought light to the dark depths of the sea bed. It shone directly onto dancing schools of brightly coloured fish, mingling lazily with the coral. Gux could not muster up any more words to express his amazement. They swam around the base of the city until they came to a huge spherical opening. The brightness that shone from within was so powerful that it temporarily blinded him. Suddenly the dolphin stopped, directly in front of them was a welcoming party of swordfish.

The swordfish were floating upright next to each other forming an archway with their sword noses, their pink bodies shone like neon beacons in the reflection of the city light.

"They are welcoming you Gux."

"I feel honoured," Gux gushed. The dolphin manoeuvred himself through the swordfish tunnel as best he could. Whilst swimming through, Gux bowed his small body in respect to each of the swordfish. Meeting them at the other side stood an imposing row of great white sharks. This could have been a very frightening experience but Gux sensed only love and peace. Each shark was holding a giant sea shell in their huge jaws. Upon seeing Gux they sounded an underwater fanfare which sent strong vibrations through the waters almost cracking Gux's fragile shell.

Gux marvelled at the underwater wonders of Virejus.

"Why does the coral shine so much?" he asked as they cruised through the intricate coral swim ways.

"When Virejus was originally built light was a big problem but they discovered a luminous plankton which formed on the ocean bed. They coated the coral with this substance and as you can see it's very effective."

The dolphin was about to tell Gux how the coral could be hollowed out for storage but he heard Gux singing and realised that he wasn't listening anyway, The dolphin didn't mind, he could see his friend had a lot to be distracted by. VIrejus must seem overwhelming to any new visitor, heck even though it was his home there were times that he found himself in awe.

The dolphin and Gux continued their journey in virtual silence; they veered into places of interest. The numerous swim-ways were cleverly lined with light coloured sponge that led to every part of the city. The entrance to each designated area was marked off according to its importance by rock archways which were dotted with plankton covered shells. The more shells on display the more important the venue was.

They passed the amphitheatre which had been built especially for the leader, the entrance of which had hundreds of shells to signify its prominence. The dolphin explained that it had taken many years to build, and form the colourful semi-circle rows of seats, each single seat had been crafted out of an individual shell.

After passing the amphitheatre they coasted by the large food farms which were needed to feed the population. Gux caught sight of one crate of prawns.

"Baba's favourite food," he shouted excitedly.

"Yes Gux everything is here, we live in perfect harmony with each other and the correct order of nature."

Each area they swam through was bustling with activity. There were tireless sting rays carrying heavy loads on their broad flat bodies, and tiny fish preening the backs of the docile looking sharks.

Amidst all of this Gux suddenly became puzzled for he had expected to see some sort of leadership directing the various operations or at the very least visible policing.

"Who is running this place?" he asked. "Who are your supervisors?"

"Ah don't worry you will find out,"

A large grey building came into view as they swam past the food farm. It stretched imposingly upwards towards the surface. The roof was cone shaped and the tip seemed to stretch into the heavens. Gux felt vibrations and soon realised that music was filtering through an oblong doorway. It seemed like a smooth and serene melody.

"Wow I can sense music" Gux gasped, "It's beautiful, what is the instrument? I haven't heard anything like it before?"

"It's a harp" replied the dolphin. It gives such a soft and clear vibration. There is a concert in there; it's where I have been told to bring you to meet our leader."

Gux felt tense at the thought of meeting the leader. What if they didn't like him? He must be so powerful to run this kingdom, how would he even know what to say to someone like that? Luckily the enchanting music helped to steady his nerves a little.

They swam inside through the huge arched doorway which was big enough for a passing great blue whale to easily glide around them. The circular room was huge, Gux felt like he was in a giant bell. They halted in the doorway, the room was crowded and there was little space to move. All forms of underwater life were there; from lobsters to clown fish, sharks to dolphins and everything in-between. Everyone was gathered around a circular stage in the centre. On stage was a purple octopus surrounded by 8 harps. He was gently brushing his tentacles against the strings to produce a heavenly sound. It was much louder now because they were both nearer, and the music seemed to bounce off the walls and travel upwards. Each note pulsated through the water. It was hypnotic to watch, it sounded like a huge harp orchestra was performing.

Gux could hardly believe his eyes, the sight was mesmerising. Out of the corner of his eye he suddenly saw something that drew his attention away from the display on the stage. The first row of spectators was sitting on exquisite seats made of pink pearls. Central to which and directly opposite Gux was an elaborate ivory white throne. It was so elegant and imposing . The back of the throne was higher than the stage canopy .

Sitting upon this beautiful object was a stately figure, at least 7 foot tall. The figure was covered in long white hair that floated gently around its body fanned by the cool ocean currents. He had a ghostly aura about him. Visible through the mane were two piercing green eyes peering out majestically at the musicians. Gux realised that this must be the leader his friend had spoken about. His curiosity for this strange creature wavered and was replaced with anxiety. Gux began to tremble.

"Don't be afraid," the dolphin said kindly sensing his friends fear." He is a wonderful being. The only thing that ever upsets him is violence and greed. You are neither violent nor greedy Gux, he will love you. In fact I know he already does."

The performance was coming to an end. As the last note played the audience burst into spontaneous cheers. The octopus paraded on the stage waving his tentacles in appreciation. He was clearly enjoying the glory. After the crowd began to lose their steam (or their voices, Gux wasn't sure which it was), they slowly started making their way out of the hall. The octopus stayed and mingled for as long as he could soaking up everyone's praise. Eventually even he had to make his way out with everyone else. Gux and the dolphin had patiently been waiting by the doorway politely nodding to those passing by as they left. The hall was soon virtually empty, it seemed so much bigger now and every small sound was amplified. Gux was almost afraid to speak.

The only one that remained seated was the leader; he had barely moved a muscle since the performance had ended. He had just continued to sit and watch as if he was still spectating. Those who had been sitting on the inner circle with him were the only other creatures there but they were talking to one another in small groups, obviously waiting for their leader to tell them when it was time to go.

"Come lets go and see him" said the dolphin excitedly. They drifted down towards the platform where the leader sat. The great, sublime figure spotted the pair and pointed in their direction making Gux feel as if a spotlight was suddenly on him.

"Why, it's my dolphin messenger and his Burabob Friend." He beckoned the pair closer with his long fingers . He then spoke in a slow yet commanding tone. "I have been waiting for you. I want to hear all about the maps."

Lome was then helped to his feet by his two personal aids. As Gux stepped off the back of his dolphin friend he felt a great calm come over him. He felt much more confident and relaxed. His mind was crystal clear. All his tortuous thoughts and memory lapses were gone as he stood in respectful silence.

Lome looked at Gux, straight in the eye. Gux didn't feel uncomfortable as one might expect. "Gux" he said gently. "You were chosen by me to do a special job. Now I want you to tell me everything about it. Just take your time, we are in no hurry. Time here in Virejus stands still. Every day is as wonderful as the next."

Lome gently placed his hand on to the small frame of Gux and stroked his shell lovingly with his delicate pointed finger nails.

"I took both maps and delivered them as you had instructed," Gux spoke naturally. The words just flowed almost as if he had no part in forming them, "No problem arose, although the swim to the Tardan land was a strenuous journey."

"What was the reaction you received from both races?" Asked Lome

"I gave the Tardan map to a scout who had been hunting on the glacier; he was definitely surprised by my appearance but said nothing. I was actually able to see the Sheerak leader and he seemed very excited by the map. He sent an exploratory craft to search the area where the cross mark was on his map. I have subsequently learnt that the craft crashed, killing the occupants."

Lome sat down again; he was silent for some time, clearly deep in thought. No one else felt the need to interrupt him. "They seem to be heading for a collision course. Hopefully some sanity will prevail but only time will tell. This is their test; they must discard their selfish and destructive emotions to free themselves from violence. This situation must be amended peacefully." Lome paused. " ...or else."

Gux looked bemused.

"Or else what?" he asked

"I have powers Gux, way beyond that of the Tardan and Sheerak. I hope they realise the errors of their ways before it's too late."

Gux already knew Lome had powers he could sense them but he didn't feel threatened by him at all. As Gux contemplated this, Lome lifted his right arm up high, he pointed towards a big tuna fish which was moving past them. From his out stretched hand, came a high-pitched vibration which cut through the water and thudded into the side of the giant tuna. The tuna skin burnt at the point of contact, it instantly died. A grotesque tuna carcass floated past Gux's eye line.

Before Gux had time to process the horrific actions he had just witnessed, Lome lifted his other arm and directed a second beam of vibrations towards the now dead fish. A light flashed which blinded all those who watched this spectacle. By the time the light had faded the tuna fish was swimming happily just as it had before. The flesh was completely undamaged. The only one who looked shocked was Gux, everyone else clearly knew that Lome wouldn't let an innocent fish die for no purpose.

"You see Gux," Lome said, "I can give life and take it away. Despite this power though, I choose to never take life senselessly. I believe life is precious; from the smallest molecule to the great leaders; everything and everyone is worthwhile."

Gux stared at Lome transfixed by his words and actions. He momentarily looked up at the great leaders face staring for any sign of protruding features but there were none. Only his large round green eyes were visible, staring out from within a wild white mane and emitting an aura of love and affection.

"Send for the flying fish!" Lome suddenly commanded. "They must increase their scouting missions into Esterevania." The dolphin swam away towards the centre of the city, instinctively carrying out his leaders command. Lome and the rest of the Virejus entourage began to make their way out of the theatre.

Once outside Lome and his two aids guided Gux to his subterranean home. As they swam together, Gux began to dread the thought of leaving this tranquil place.

"Do you want to speak to me Gux?" Lome asked, as if he could read minds.

"Your life here is so tranquil." Gux replied. "I would be honoured if I ever had the chance to stay here."

"You wouldn't miss your own people?" Lome asked.

"Maybe a little,"Gux answered hesitantly, "but I think I would miss this place more."

"Peaceful creatures are always welcome here. I suggest that you return to your people before making a decision though. A move here is permanent and you cannot make this decision in haste. If you still feel the same, after some time we would be delighted to accept you. "He put a warm hand on Gux's shoulder. "Today, you will leave with the dolphin. When I feel the time is right I will send him back to collect you. If you want to come back that is." Gux squealed with delight, he was ecstatic. He had never dreamt of a place so perfect before, he was sure he would return.

"I think I'd stay just to avoid the jeel," Gux laughed. Lome lifted his arm, bringing his effortless swimming action to a slow halt.

"The jeel," he said thoughtfully, "I have heard about this creature from the flying fish. Am I right to say they are located on the surface of the ocean, like a membrane jelly?"

"Yes Lome, it is deadly though," Gux felt his contented feeling become disrupted at the mere thought of the jeel. "It can swallow a Burabob up; I was nearly killed the other day."

"We shall deal with this Jeel," Lome announced. "We cannot have this sort of danger threatening your kind people. Maybe we can find another place in the ocean where it can live in isolation"

Gux was once again in awe of Lome. The jeel had been such a dark cloud over the Burabob and this great leader was able to offer a solution so quickly . Gux had a feeling that the problem had been eliminated at that very moment although he was sure that was impossible.

They arrived at the residence of Lome, Gux was disappointed. He expected it to be grand but it was nothing stupendous at all. It was smaller than some of the other houses Gux had seen. It was however beautifully decorated. The outside was completely covered in garlands of underwater Lily's intertwined skilfully over the mushroom shaped residence.

"I like colour," He announced to Gux, as he guided him through the stemmed coral structure of the home. They followed a small coral stairway up and up in to the main umbrella of the dome shaped place. It had a bright yellow floor made from strong reeds. At one side of the room lay oyster shells strewn about in an untidy fashion. Some oysters still had pearls in them but the others were lying on a small snakeskin covered table by the doorway.

"You look curious my friend?" Lome said

"Sorry, I just expected you to have a home of great opulence. You have very few commodities, except for those magnificent pearls of course". Lome paused before he spoke.

"There are few luxuries in my home Gux, after all who needs them. To be inwardly content is more important. The pearls are my only luxury; they are items of beauty that I appreciate. I do not collect them to be greedy but simply to admire. They help me recognise the beauty of the world."

"Burabob dwellings have a lot of precious things but they are only for the purpose of improving our homes, we are not greedy either."

"Yes Gux I knew you would understand." Lome seemed excited. "It is fine to have nice things around. Why look at our intricate and beautiful city. We appreciate beautiful things; In fact it is a sign of an advanced civilisation. However it is what one does and how one acquires wealth that can be a problem. I know the Burabob are peace makers and gentle creatures that's why only you could deliver the maps. Your people have nothing to fear. All peacemakers will be looked after, regardless of what species they are." Lome sat down on the reed floor, Gux sat beside him. Gux felt at ease sitting next to Lome despite his awesome presence and clear physical power. It was in fact nicer for Gux because their height difference didn't seem so big while sitting.

"I have to ask," Gux braved. "What is the reason for the maps?"

"It is simply a test." Lome replied. "I have created a situation that will appeal to the greedy and violent side of both species. If they refuse the bait good enough, if not then these maps will prove what we have been getting reports on for quite some time now. There have been hostilities all over Esterevania. It saddens me so much especially when I see the heartache that this conflict causes. We are underwater hybrids but this evolutionary and physical transformation does nothing to quell the spirit and purpose of our people that stretches back for many generations. We have been aware of the Sheerak's and Tardan's for an eternity and have watched over their developments. They could be so much better if they learnt to live in peace. This will be the ultimate test."

"What do you mean when you say the peace making people will be OK?"

"That will be answered later." Lome said calmly." You must be patient Gux. I promise that whatever happens we will guarantee your peoples safety. If hostilities spread to your peaceful homes on the beach then I will intervene. I have told my scouts to inform me if anything of this nature occurs."

Gux's dolphin friend came back accompanied by 6 brightly coloured fish.

"Take Gux back to his people." Lome instructed. "I am sure we will see him again as he has plans to join us here. I have granted his wish."

The dolphin bellowed in delight. "Wonderful. Then I can really show you the ocean."

"Now my flying fish," Lome announced in a loud voice. The six silver fish swam near to his side expectantly. "Your mission is very important, you must gain all the information we need and keep a low profile. You will report on any hostilities as often as you can." The fish bowed their heads one after the other as a gesture of respect towards their leader.

It was time for Gux to leave. He bowed his head just as the fish had and waved goodbye. He didn't feel sad anymore because he knew in his heart he would be back.

They swam down through Lome's home and out into the clear waters of Virejus. They left the main city entrance and Gux began to shiver. He was reminded of how cold the real world was in comparison with his future home. Despite how he felt on the outside, inside, his heart remained warm like Virejus.

CHAPTER 22

ACTION STATIONS

Nepht eased his dart into a gentle decline touching down safely on Salak's gleaming marble landing pad. As he made his way towards the palace he could almost taste bile in his throat. He knew he would have to fake some concern about the death of Etar and this thought turned his stomach.

A loud gong signalled to Salak that Nepht had arrived; he assumed Etar was with him. Salak had spent the last hour pacing and muttering, he suddenly turned impatiently towards the door waiting for the pair's entrance.

Nepht came in with his eyes on the floor trying his best to look solemn. Salak could sense something was wrong; "What is it?" he asked frantically, "where is Etar?"

Nepht forced out a long sigh and looked up at his incompetent leader. "Etar has been killed." Salak stepped back in shock. "A Tardan gun shot him down."

"Those Tardan animals," Salak's face twisted in disbelief.

"They retaliated after I had killed two of their people," Nepht said calmly, smiling inside because he knew Salak would hate this news.

"You did what?" Salak predictably screamed.

"I had to, it was an uneasy situation. It was either us or them. We are strong and should show ourselves to be warriors."

Salak sat down dejected. There was no point arguing with Nepht. Etar was dead, war was imminent and he was tired of it all.

Nepht could feel frustration building inside him, the feebleness of Salak had never been more obvious, his body was slumped and his face sad. He should be angry thought Nepht.

"We need those maps Sir, those riches should be ours," he prompted knowing someone had to take leadership.

After a few moments of awkward silence Salak stood up slightly more energised. "Right" he said, "This is the situation and if it can't be changed then we must move forward. Let's get ready for battle then. You must go now and give the orders. As soon as the battle crafts are ready we will launch. Our only chance is to surprise the Tardan." Salak felt a little more like his old self now he was commanding a war.

In his heart though he knew this wasn't what he wanted. He no longer had the appetite for blood shed, he wasn't confident he was even capable of it anymore. He just thought that if he kept pretending no one would notice. Nepht had noticed.

"Now go Nepht and remember; now we are not just fighting for victory but our very existence." Nepht scoffed he knew this already and it excited him.

As Nepht made his way out of the palace and back to his dart he continued to plot his take over. He knew that he needed to get Salak out of the safety of the palace and into the air again. It wasn't going to be easy. Salak was a proficient and enthusiastic flyer in his hey day but for years now he had remained in his palace, he had aged a great deal and was no longer the vision of warrior strength he once was.

Nepht guessed that, and he knew it. If he could just talk Salak into flying a mission then he would have his chance. He racked his brain to think of how he could entice Salak out. He continued on his mission and arrived at the construction base, he made his way straight for the microphone. He may not be in charge yet, but he relished being the one to announce imminent war.

Nepht abruptly pulled the microphone out from the hands of the operator,

"Now here this," his echoing voice brought the place to a standstill "This is Red Alert. I repeat Red Alert. You need to make the battle crafts ready for immediate flight. A Tardan marksman has shot down one of our darts and killed Etar. This was an act of war. We must protect our species."

There was a deadly shocked silence before the construction area suddenly exploded into life. Machine workers dashed about in all directions. There was a panicked but charged atmosphere. A crescendo of noise erupted as all the engines in the battle fleet seemed to fire up at once filling the air with a distinct acidic vapour. Within 10 minutes two distinct lines of streamlined red darts were lined up on the twin launch pads.

It may have been a long time since an order like that had been given but the Sheerak were always ready and waiting for the next opportunity to fight. Years ago it had been with each other but Salak had united the species after winning a tremendous battle and wiping out his Sheerak enemy completely. Despite this, the appetite for war had not depleted in the hearts of many Sheerak's.

Nepht watched proudly, Salak was fortunate to have such well-prepared committed fighters. Soon they would be under his command though. He glanced through the looking glass which disrupted his good feeling; the sight of his reflection wearing Sala's disgusting red flying suit made him nauseous. He tugged at the epaulettes emblazoned with Salak's emblem. He started to feel better again as he imagined his own emblem instead. He gathered his composure and made his way down from the elevated viewing box. He made straight for the awaiting Gyrospheres beckoning the chief pilot. He then had an idea.

"I want you to contact Salak," he commanded. "Ask him if he would like to accompany us aboard the Gyrosphere for he may want to watch the battles in action. Remind him the Gyrosphere is quite safe."

"Yes sir," said the chief pilot. If he wondered about Nepht's sincerity he certainly didn't dare question it. Nepht watched as the pilot strode energetically towards the communications room .He was feeling anxious about his plan. He nervously waited, pulling at his baggy trousers with his giant claws. The material was so thin he almost ripped through it in agitation. He then looked up to see the chief pilot returning again. The thick wrinkled skin on his face was etched with a disappointed frown.

"Salak would rather wait at the palace. He said we should keep him informed of developments."

Inside Nepht screamed. Outwardly though, he contained his anger.

"Give the order to take off." he said to the pilot plainly as if Salak's presence was of no real importance. "Make haste towards Tardan territory, destroy anything that moves. I will follow you later, I have business to finish here beforehand." The pilot nodded and took control of the launch.

Nepht watched as the proud Sheerak war machine lifted into the air. The Gyrosphere was an awesome sight to behold; it lifted off the ground effortlessly gliding upwards in a majestic motion. The twin Gyroscopes started to spin silently within their main structured frames .

.The blinding sun reflected off the golden metal momentarily blinding Nepht. Soon after start up the sound of these rotating machines created a deafening roar that seemed to vibrate Sheerak bones. As the ships flew into the distance, one thought dominated Nepht's angry mind; Salak .

CHAPTER 23

THE BUBBLE BURSTS

Rostia and Erith patiently waited at the bottom of the stairs to the city.

"Surely they won't be much longer now." Rostia moaned.

"They have been away for quite some time now. I hope everything went well." Erith said feeling a little anxious. A shaft of light pierced down towards them bringing their conversation to a halt.

Gradually their eyes became accustomed to the bright daylight rays spreading over the top of them until they could see the small figures descending the stairway. Rostia noticed straight away that something wasn't right. She anxiously gripped Erith's arm.

"There seems to be two men missing."

"They must be following behind," replied Erith measuredly. They both searched the figures, waiting to see the whole party.

"I can't see Eli" Rostia eventually said, Erith had realised this before but was afraid to say, "I can't see Eli." She repeated panicked. Erith put her arm around Rostia's frail shoulders. They braced themselves for bad news.

Orsov walked towards them dejectedly. He looked directly into Rostia's eyes; his tears betrayed his stubborn silence. Rostia looked at his forlorn expression and knew instinctively why her soul mate wasn't there. Time seemed to stand still; her heart felt like a razor sharp knife had pierced straight through it. She was on the verge of being sick.

Orsov took her small trembling hand and held it close to his heart. The two stared at each other; both knowing what had been so far unsaid. For a few moments they existed in a bubble, afraid to speak the truth in case it made the whole nightmare real.

"Please," Rostia eventually begged, "please, say it isn't so."

"I'm sorry," Orsov said shaking his head. "Eli is dead."

Rostia broke away from her tender embrace with Orsov, the bubble had been broken with the truth she had already known. She became suddenly hysterical, sobbing uncontrollably. She fell to the floor, the grief became too much for her to stand up. The others stood helplessly around her. The only audible sound was Rostia's wails.

Erith wanted to wrap her arms around Orsov, grateful that he was the one delivering the bad news and not the one missing. The two exchanged meaningful looks but neither felt it was appropriate to embrace the other in front of Rostia, instead they quietly reached out and held hands. The sense of touch between them was electric. Tears filled up Erith's eyes as she resisted holding him any closer; instead she sat down next to her new friend and wrapped her arms around her. They sat on the floor together and shared tears.

"It was a Sheerak attack he didn't stand a chance. Yond too was killed." Wok said loudly so he could be heard over the sobbing. "He died fighting for his people." This was supposed to be reassuring but it prompted an angry look from Orsov.

"Many of our friends have died in the same way. Is it not about time we realised it is all so futile."

"This is different, we have made peace as Tardan's but we cannot negotiate with the reptile Sheerak's. They fired at us without provocation. They killed two of our men, they will pay. The fight continues."

Orsov didn't care why this had happened he didn't care whose fault it was but after years of conflict the one thing he had learnt was that violence only created more violence.

Wok interrupted Orsov's reflections. "I want to know more about the Sheerak's .

"Is that all you think about Wok, your own ends? I thought for a while that you had changed. When you said those words in the cave before the battle of the Nardi Glacier, I really believed you, I really did. But now, all I see is the old Wok, the distant and aloof dictator. I see that look in your eye, you love this, and you love the bloodshed of war. Will you ever learn?"

Erith stood by her husband, recognising that however right he was and how ever close to Wok he was, angering their leader was never a good idea. "We need to stay calm," she said directing her words as much at Orsov as Wok. Rostia is clearly distressed and now is not the time for this debate or for battle plans"

"Distressed" mocked Wok. "Look I'm sorry he died, I am sorry anyone has to die but its life. This is the right time and if Rostia is too sensitive to deal with it then she needs to get out of my sight. We have work to do and a war to win."

His voice was full of hate. He despised being dictated to by a female and Orsov was doing nothing to control her, in fact his subordination was even worse. He was supposed to be able to count on him for support, his disrespect was unacceptable. He realised that there were dozens of spectators witnessing this argument. He became even more enraged. He had to act.

"I will have you and your supporters detained until you see a bit more sense." He announced.

"Detained!" screamed Orsov, Wok snapped his fingers and within seconds his guards appeared.

"Take these three to the detention unit." He waved his hands indicating Orsov, Erith and Rostia. "Anybody else who wants to join them is welcome."

Consternation broke out as Orsov was seized by two guards. He fought fiercely to free himself but he was bludgeoned to the ground by the butt of a laser gun. Erith dropped to her knees beside him. She looked up at Wok, pleading.

"How can you do this to him, he has been so loyal to you."

"It is his history of loyalty that is saving his life right now. If he changes his attitude I will free you all."

Erith tried to wipe oozing blood from Orsov's battered head but she too was dragged to her feet and held by two guards. Rostia simply stood there rooted to the spot she had no fight left in her.

"Why are you punishing Rostia? Erith questioned in a disgusted tone. She looked at Wok, searching for a small sign of compassion but there was none. "What about the words from the treaty. You gave a promise that this new Tardan society would not degenerate into this sort of behaviour."

Wok didn't even answer her ignoring her completely.

"Take them away guards. I don't want any more trouble from them." Orsov was dragged limply between two guards. Erith and Rostia too were jostled and finally pushed in the direction of the Detention centre.

The crowds had grown around them during the altercation and now it seemed as if the whole of the city stood silent observing this leadership conflict. Murmurings began to filter through the onlookers but nobody else dared to speak out.

CHAPTER 24

DETENTION

The detention centre itself was nothing more than a filthy cage. A stale odour was evident as the threesome was thrown unceremoniously to the ground. Erith instinctively held her stomach protecting her unborn child. Erith and Rostia sat Orsov against the steel bars surrounding them. Erith ripped a piece of her pigskin dress and tried to stop the flow of blood still ebbing from the deep scar on his forehead.

His eyes gradually opened, his blood caked lips parted, revealing the charming Orsov smile. His white teeth sparkled as she flung her arms around his neck.

"For one awful moment I thought you had lapsed into a coma." Erith burst into tears of relief.

Orsov struggled to laugh, stopping to cough and catch his breath. "I've never been able to sleep well, I am not about to start now."

Orsov and Erith embraced, they held each other tight as if holding on to the remains of their future, to hope, to love. They had held back earlier after Orsov's return so as not to upset Rostia but their own emotional turmoil had become too much, but in that moment they no longer thought of anyone or anything but each other.

Rostia sat with her back on the other side of the cage. She felt as if she was invading their privacy all of a sudden. Looking at them made her heart feel heavy like lead. She understood they needed this embrace but it still felt like salt in her fresh wounds. She held her head in her knees, trying to stifle her tears but her shoulders shook giving her grief away.

Erith was suddenly aware of her surroundings and of Rostia, she turned to see her and felt instant guilt. She and Orsov looked at each other speaking a thousand words with one glance.

"Rostia," Erith said gently leaving Orsov's side, "We are so sorry,"

"When this is all over," Orsov said gently, "you will be part of our family. We will take care of you. I owe it to my friend to look after you." His words were sincere but in reality none of them knew if they would see the day that this was all over anyway.

Rostia looked up. She had known this couple for the shortest time but that seemed so irrelevant now. Their generosity and kind spirit was plain to see. Despite her enormous loss she did feel loved. They both smiled at her and she smiled too. It was the first time she had felt her grief ease even if it was momentarily.

At the other end of the city Wok had already summoned the remainder of his battle commanders to his palace and was preparing his battle orders. Tak and Lato sat unnerved and still stunned by the imprisonment of Orsov.

"My warriors look so glum," Wok eventually said, acknowledging the strange atmosphere. "Is there a problem may I ask?"

There was silence.

"What is the problem?" Wok repeated shouting this time.

There was silence

"Why did you do it?" Tak suddenly said, it was almost a whisper but Wok heard.

"Do you want to join your friend ?"

Tak shifted uncomfortably in his seal skin chair. "I just want an answer that's all. Orsov was your right hand man."

"Discipline my dear Tak, discipline. It has been sadly lacking in our community recently. Orsov forced me to make an example of him; he is to blame not me."

Tak tried to get eye contact from Lato for support but Lato kept his eyes firmly at the ground.

"Anyone else have any questions?" Wok asked sarcastically. It was almost a challenge.

Once again there was silence.

"Good, now let me see the Pendurotor that Revar has conceived, is it ready for battle?"

"Almost," Lato responded, relieved the conversation had returned to technology where he was far more comfortable. "It can be assembled as soon as you wish. The two main components of each machine are ready and waiting."

"Will it take long to assemble?

"No, there is an integral locking device."

"Good. Let's engage battle procedure right away."

Tak and Lato looked at each other shocked at the speed things were moving.

"Lato, you stay here to help me with strategic planning. Everyone else must go." Wok dismissed everyone waving his arms. Lato did not want to stay but he dare not argue.

Moments after Tak had left Thori and Revar arrived.

"We've heard the news." Thori said angrily.

"Don't worry Thori, I am preparing to attack the Sheerak. They will not get away with it."

"Not that," retorted Thori "I'm talking about the imprisonment of Orsov."

"Oh that," Wok laughed.

"What is going on?" Thori banged his fist on the table.

"Orsov spoke of rebellion, I will not allow it."

"Rebellion? From what I heard he only wanted peace. How is it rebellious to want peace?"

"Peace is not an option. I am the leader and I say we are at war. If he does not support me he is rebellious."

"If my memory serves me right our Treaty was signed to curb such an incident." Revar edged over to Thori's side and tugged at his black sealskin cape. He wanted to stop Thori before he said something he might regret. The last thing the Tardan's needed now was to start fighting against each other again.

"Let's make this clear shall we," said Wok, "we will fight the Sheerak. Will you fight by my side Thori or are you also organising a rebellion?"

"Whatever is the right or wrong thing to do regarding the Sheerak is irrelevant to me right now, it is you that I have a bigger problem with. We are supposed to be a team, to make decisions together. I am not prepared to be bullied into war."

"Guards," screamed Wok.

"Take him away as well. Put him next to the people he loves so dearly." There was an audible shock from those around them.

Brandishing their lasers menacingly the palace guards surrounded Thori.

Ah so that's it remove the thorns from beneath so you can trample more easily" scowled Thori.

"Take him away get him out of my sight." Wok waved his arms unconcernedly.

"You won't keep us down forever you know," Thori shouted as he was being dragged away. His voice was suddenly stifled as a stainless steel nozzle from one of the guard's laser guns had prodded harshly against the bottom of his jaw.

Revar stood there dumbstruck. It had all happened so quickly.

"Come my dear friend" Wok gestured to Revar. "I knew you would see sense. Sit beside Lato, I want to discuss battle plans.

There were several moments of awkward silence, so much had happened in such a short space of time it was hard to simply ignore. The surrounding crystal décor glistened intermittently, emitting bursts of colour which soothed the uneasy silence. Wok spoke first.

"Now Revar, do you think we should attack the heart of the Sheerak land or do you think we should be cautious and make forays to their outlying posts?" The sculptured index finger of Revar's delicate hand rubbed up and down his stretched almost ghostly features.

"I don't think you would accomplish anything with the second option once we attacked their outlying posts it would only give them a warning of our intentions. No I think we should head straight for the nerve centre of the Sheerak people. That way we should surprise them and hopefully retrieve the maps intact."

Lato nodded in agreement. "Yes it sounds like the best idea."

Wok stood up and paced around swinging his long strong arms to and fro. He lifted one of his long drooping ears and scratched inside. His thoughts came to a halt.

"Yes your option seems to be the best but our battle machines have not been exposed to the extreme climate of the Sheerak. What if they fail at the important moment? At least attacking their perimeter would give us an idea of our capabilities."

"Our machines have been tested for heat resistance with lasers. You can't get a better test than that. Furthermore we must attack with decisiveness. We cannot afford to waste time."

Revar's confident answer excited Wok; he banged his hairy fists against the table.

"Let's do it" he shouted feeling the adrenalin course through his veins. Wok had always felt most alive with the prospect of impending death. Any doubts he had secretly harboured over the last few hours were gone. He was sure he was doing the right thing.

He was the leader of all the Tardan's now Thori had been imprisoned. Once they had defeated the Sheerak he would rule alone. The thought of all the power made him giddy with pure pleasure. He would become a god. Any softening emotions from the past few weeks were gone; the situation with the maps, the riches and the Sheerak's had reminded him of his true self.

"Now we shall change into battle dress and prepare for attack." He said and simply walked out the room, muttering to his guards to prepare his armour. Lato and Revar were left alone together. They slowly and awkwardly followed Wok out to prepare themselves for a battle they never thought they would be fighting.

Wok had returned to his dressing room. The guards began to dress him, as they had done many times before. First they fitted the high polished waistcoat. Wok glanced at it briefly. It always made him feel good to see its perfect shine. Next they fitted his battle trousers. Wok grumbled as he always did at this bit, he hated forcing on these tight fitting leggings but they protected his flesh which he appreciated. Once the leggings had been clipped to the waistcoat he stepped into his spiked battle boots. Then they fitted the steel meshed outer protective jacket and gauntlets. Finally the guards handed over his favourite helmet. It provided the necessary all round protection especially the dropped sides which covered his long dangling ears It also provided ample vision because of the open face which was strengthened by two horizontal support bars. He carefully pressed the helmet over his strong head and neck but he scratched his small flat nose with one of the bars in the helmet making his eyes water.

"How do I look?" he asked his guards, knowing they would only give a positive answer out of fear. Wok liked that feeling.

"You look like a splendid and strong leader" said one of the guards.

"As I expected," he scoffed "Now sound the fanfare. Let everyone know we are at war."

The two guards disappeared and within moments Wok, along with all the other Tardan's could hear the brass horns which made an incessant high note that signalled war.

The noise carried all the way to the detention centre.

"Do you hear that? " Orsov said sadly. "It is war again. I've grown to hate that sound."

"Don't worry my friend." Reassured their new cell mate Thori. "We will find a way to peace again. It is my mission. These bars may hold my body but my spirit is high. We cannot let Wok nor the Sheerak take our hope. When we believe that there is a future, our souls will search for a way to make it so. If we believe we are defeated we will find nothing but evidence of our loss. I have learnt so much in the past few weeks, of this I am certain."

After Wok had mounted his polar bear for the short journey to the city elevators, he gestured to his drummers who were resplendent in all white suits and matching drum kits. They contrasted perfectly with the alternate rows of brown leather suited warriors.

All the Tardan's from the city had now gathered on each side of the perimeter road. The atmosphere was not the same as it had been on previous tribal battles. Most of the general public had no real idea what it was about and whatever had caused this sudden need for battle. Wok was so caught up in himself and the mission he hadn't even explained it. All they knew was that Orsov had disagreed. No one dared to question Wok so they went through the motions as he would expect them to. Wok felt in his heart that it wasn't the same. He knew that he didn't have the same enthusiastic support but he ignored it. Choosing to focus on the anger he held inside, the anger that always served him so well in war.

The drum and trumpet beats grew all the time until finally Wok was at the entrance again. The army fanfare stopped when they reached the elevators. Tak, Revar and Lato stood there in readiness.

"Ah my trusted chiefs, you look magnificent in your battle armour." This somewhat derisive comment was made knowing full well that his three Noran commanders hated the idea of covering up their humanoid streamlined bodies. Their plasticised bodies were built for speed and the armour only made them feel uncomfortable.

"Are the machines ready?" Wok asked

"Yes Wok all 20 of them are working perfectly" said Revar

"Excellent, I want to send two waves of battle machines. I will travel at the head of the first battle wave formation along with you Revar. Tak and Lato will follow in the second wave."

A faint buzzing noise enticed Woks gaze, his mouth fell open as he watched the huge Pendurotors roll forward towards the elevator. Once the first of the two spherical Pendurotors had reached the elevator they stopped and the flashing colours from within gradually died down.

"It's time to board. We only need a dozen men to each machine" said Tak

"Is that all?" queried Wok

"Yes, for everything is computerised," confirmed Revar. It dawned on Revar how unprepared they were, it was incomprehensible that they were having this discussion now, minutes before take-off. Wok turned to address his army.

"We only need a dozen men to each sphere. The rest of my army will be deployed in and around the city to protect it. Reassemble the rocket launchers and make ready the Takus machines in case they are needed."

Wok turned around again and stared at the huge spheres in awe.

"Amazing simply amazing," he gasped, "they must be all of thirty metres in diameter."

"Thirty two point five to be precise," said Revar proudly.

"What are the indentations on the outside of the spheres?"

"They protrude through the outer shell to a predetermined length. Giving added grip whilst the sphere is on the surface. Even more importantly the tips of these protrusions are spiked enabling the sphere to pierce and crush whilst on the ground too."

"Those reptiles will have nothing this superior. We will surely crush them."

A short while after the first wave of spheres had been manned and their nervous pilots had edged them into position on the enormous elevator pads Tak sounded a clearance Klaxon and then pressed the elevator button.

The huge platform gently lifted. It raised effortlessly higher revealing two transparent power rams. They were flashing an ever lengthening turquoise colour. Suddenly there was a small jolt and the platform stopped. A square section of the undergrounds city's canopy slid back revealing the bright pink sky. The hydraulic sequence once again continued until all the spheres were through the roof.

As they had been instructed by Revar the pilot pressed the vertical lift thrusts and slowly but surely the Pendurotor lifted up moving forward at the same time. It increased in speed as the pendulum built up momentum. Revar looked through the transparent viewing panel and set their designated course.

CHAPTER 25

THE DREAM BECOMES A REALITY

Nepht arrived at Salak's palace and brushed by the startled guard giving him no chance to sound the entrance gong. Salak was slouched over his throne sleeping. His pet leopards lay sleeping protectively at his webbed feet. They opened their eyes instinctively knowing that Salak had company but when they saw Nepht they knew there wasn't any danger.

Without a sound they stealthily stood up stretching first their front legs and then their hind. This gradual yet athletic movement aroused Salak from his sleep. His deep set eyes flickered in surprise. He stroked his rough face irritably, still not aware of Nepht's presence.

"Salak," said Nepht in an abrupt manner startling his leader.

"How did you get inside without the guard seeing you?"

"I tried to stop him Salak" said the guard following behind Nepht apologetically.

Nepht ignored the guard completely.

"I want to know the reason why you are not accompanying our battle fleet?"

"'I've already explained this to you, I need to be here in my palace?"

Nepht spread his reptilian legs in a threatening gesture "Is there something else you're hiding?"

"I'm not hiding anything and furthermore I do not have to explain anything to you. Now please leave the palace and return to your battle position."

"It's not because you are a coward is it?" Nepht knew this was it. He had officially overstepped the mark. He could not go back now.

"Did I hear you correctly Nepht?" Salak was puzzled as to why his trusted warrior would say such a thing. It felt like a kick in the stomach, made worse by the fact that Salak knew it was true.

"Yes you heard me, a coward." Salak pushed himself up from his throne saying nothing. He lumbered to the doorway and spoke calmly to the guard. He realised that finally he had been caught out. He had tried to hide his incompetence but now Nepht knew. Salak foresaw what was about to happen but he resolved he wasn't going to go down without a fight; one last fight.

"Take my two pets out of here and close the entrance behind you." He calmly instructed.

"You think you can do my job and lead my people do you?"

"Yes" screamed Nepht. "You were once great but it is time you stepped down. I should be king not you."

"I will not go quietly" smiled Salak, feeling alive for the first time in years.

Suddenly, in rage Nepht lunged for his laser but Salak saw him and responded fiercely. He swung his arm up and round in a great loop, slicing into Nepht's face tearing apart his jaw and cheekbone leaving it gaping and spurting with blood. Nepht staggered backwards falling over a golden vase by the doorway.

The stumble eased his grip and he dropped his laser to the floor. Salak moved swiftly. He took another great swing and sank his claw into Nepht's side piercing through Nepht's flying suit and deep into his internal organs.

Nepht let out a roar in agony as he fell to the floor. He quickly realised that he had been lucky; when he rolled over his claw came into contact with the dislodged laser. As Salak moved in for the kill Nepht grasped the laser with both claws and holding it up in the front of his lacerated face. He painfully pointed it in the direction of the menacing figure of Salak, hovering over him.

For a moment Nepht thought of all that Salak had taught him and given him over the years. Salak used to be an incredible strong leader but now he had degenerated and it was not the time for sentimentality. In that same moment Salak knew that this was the end and the truth is he actually felt relief. He no longer needed to pretend.

The blast hit Salak at point black range completely dismembering his body sending an ocean of scaled tissue splattering all over the palace. The remainder of Salak's torso lay there spewing blood in an erratic fashion, forming a wild picture of violent death upon the magnificent palace rug.

Nepht struggled to his feet as the palace guards burst in through the door, they momentarily paused, aghast at the terrible bloody site in front of them. Nepht took this opportunity and pulled the trigger on his laser twice in rapid succession. The two white beams sliced through into the guards completely tearing the head off one of them and shearing through the torso of the other. Both bodies fell to the floor together in a mangled heap. Nepht was raging with adrenalin; he continued to fire indiscriminately around the palace, destroying all of Salak's treasures that he had considered so important.

Lastly he smashed the communications board in to fragments with his fist. For a moment he paused. Breathing heavily as the enormity of the last 5 minutes began to sink in. He became very aware that his next moves had to be carefully thought through. He edged his way to the doorway and carefully checked outside but he couldn't see anyone. It seemed the palace was empty. Salak's insistence on having just two guards at the palace was now playing perfectly into the hands of Nepht, it originally was a money saving gesture from a king too tight to spend his treasures.

He moved warily up the stairs, his injuries started to really hurt as the initial adrenalin wore off. His pulse raced again though when he looked at the top of the stairs to see Salak's pet leopards. He made a forlorn attempt to aim the laser again but was relieved to see that the two leopards just went straight past him and towards the remains of Salak. They began to eat and tear frantically through the smouldering flesh.

Although Nepht had been wounded he was lucky in a way for both wounds were in the upper part of his body, he still had good use of his legs. He headed towards his parked dart and fumbled through his emergency injury kit. He found the gelatine oil which would contain his wounds temporarily. As he tended to himself he noticed the Scouts dart parked up on the other side of the landing pad. He had seen no sign of him in the palace and he didn't have time to find him now but the scout was bound to have seen the bloody mess Nepht had left behind, he couldn't risk being followed. There was only one solution he could think of; he limped over to the other parked dart and sat awkwardly into the pilot seat. He reached out and set the delayed action timer to five minutes He also pressed the self-destruction sequence.

He dragged himself away as fast as he could but as he entered his own craft he started to panic. He had caught his flying suit on the integral stairway. He tugged frantically at the flying suit until it suddenly burst free throwing him backwards into his cockpit. His heartbeat raced whilst he set the take-off sequence into operation.

Moments later the dart surged upwards and into the sky Nepht heaved a sigh of relief as he set course for the construction complex. A blinding flash accompanied by a tremendous explosion boomed behind him. It rocked the aircraft but he was unconcerned. He started to smile and the smile turned into a laugh. He had done it, he had been successful. He was in charge now. He would be king.

It was time to action the next phase of the plan. He picked up the dart's radio.

"There has been a coup at the palace by the guards but everything is now under control. Unfortunately Salak has been killed during the fighting so I will automatically assume command. I will now join the main fleet and we will still recover the maps safely." He paused for a moment deep in thought, "do not send reinforcements to the palace the situation is being dealt with."

There was silent shock from the other end of the radio.

Nepht hoped that they bought what he was saying .

CHAPTER 26

NEEDLESS SLAUGHTER

"What about our vision? It seems somewhat limited from this elevated position in the sphere."

Revar looked at Wok with a blank expression. He hated it when those inferior to his intellect made such thoughtless comments.

"Of course we have an alternative view; there is a button there that says so" Revar's sarcasm was apparent.

"Yes I see it now" laughed Wok, looking at the button clearly stating ALTERNATIVE VIEW"

"Well press it," urged Revar. Wok pressed the black button and was amazed to see a succession of outer sheath doors slide back beneath him, affording a panoramic view of the terrain directly below them. Revar activated another sequence which closed the doors beneath them and opened more at the side.

"Better?" taunted Revar.

"Yes quite satisfactory" Wok replied sheepishly. "How long will it be till we reach the Mountains?" He asked changing the subject."

"Any moment now" replied Revar.

They both stood at the viewing platform waiting patiently for any sign of the enemy. Whilst watching the glaciers beneath them sparkle like huge diamonds. Wok thought about Tak and Lato and hoped that they were getting ready with the second wave attack.

Simultaneously they both heard a faint buzzing sound and instinctively looked at the scanners for any clues as to what it was. A smile gradually etched its way over Woks tough skin.

"Ah good it's the other Pendurotors, they seem to be in perfect formation."

Revar pressed the communications button .

"Right everyone; I want you to demonstrate the colour code for distress. As Wok and Revar waited, the Spheres alongside them suddenly lit up in a bright pink haze.

"Good now revert back to a light green" ordered Revar. The spheres seemed to do as they were told.

"Excellent now we are ready." He looked at Wok smirking. "It's just another idea I came up with. The pink haze is a protective gas. It will seal off the explosive areas whilst telling us that there has been a direct hit."

"Good thinking Revar,"said Wok trying to hide his sense of awe. "Now these buttons here, are they the lasers?"

"Yes to fire you press the top row. To extend lasers for grip and spiking you press the bottom row. Each individual button corresponds with a different laser. It's a very simple process." His last comment was another small dig at the Tardan's lack of intellect but luckily Wok didn't notice.

The bright marble like glaciers of the Mountains came into view; they almost paled into insignificance against the austere light brown volcanic peeks.

"Are they not a formidable sight?" Revar said gently lifting the Pendurotor into a higher altitude.

"Have you got the map?" Wok asked. Revar stretched down and reached inside his hide boots.

"Here it is," he murmured trying to hide his irritation at Wok's obsession.

Wok opened it as if it were made of gold dust, "the cross mark on the Sheerak land seems to be in a direct line with this cluster of high peaked mountains we are approaching." He observed.

"Yes I memorised the position." Revar gloated.

Wok shuffled uncomfortably, Revar gave him a puzzling stare, "I am just very aware that the Sheerak's might be on high alert. We must monitor the terrain more closely." He shook his head in frustration, obviously not believing the ship he travelled in offered a good enough visual perspective. Revar smiled, pressed the retract buttons for the outer sheaths and with a slight jolt all four doors slid back leaving only a transparent barrier. This gave the occupants a 360° viewpoint. .

"Are the transparent shields strong?" Wok asked still looking nervous and nowhere near as impressed as Revar had expected him to be.

"There is no need to worry." He said plainly. "It is pure drathon. Shall I activate lasers too so we are ready?"

"Yes do that Revar."

All 25 laser ejection buttons were pressed sending the spiked lasers out to full extremity. The spheres were now drifting further and further into Sheerak territory. They continually altered altitude in readiness for the expected attack. Suddenly a loud roar of engines made Revar and Wok look to their right.

It's one of the Sheerak craft probably one of their scouts. "We must put him out of action before he relays a message," shouted Wok anxiously.

The dart sped by the Pendurotors at great velocity. It travelled straight for half a mile before turning abruptly. The Sheerak pilot radioed the battle headquarters.

"Tardan battle fleet located three miles inside the eastern sector of the mountains will commence attack."

Revar watched intently as the dart turned and then hurtled towards them. The dark backdrop of the mountains silhouetted the bright red dart perfectly making it an easy target. Revar pressed all rear lasers. The beams flashed simultaneously honing in mercilessly on the helpless dart. The dart disintegrated in a blinding flash sending a spray of tiny particles cascading on to the rich green undergrowth below them. Wok and Revar danced a jig of delight.

"Got him!" they both cried in unison,

The commander of the three sheerak Gyrospheres looked at his assistant and then stared down at his gleaming silver scales.

"I fear our scout has been killed. His computer has gone dead." He said sombrely. "We must be aware of the Tardan battle capabilities; I fear we underestimate them at our peril. Contact Nepht and let him know of the Tardan position."

Nepht was almost upon his battle fleet when he received the news about the scout. "I will be with you in a few moments" he replied without a hint of emotion. In truth he was excited; the fight was on and he was in charge. He carefully stroked his scales, he felt relieved that he had discarded his red flying suit. He no longer needed to hide. After the battle he planned on destroying all clothing material; Nepht was a proud reptile. The stale odour from his dripping sweat filtered through his brightly lit cockpit as he took a deep contented breath.

His radar computer flashed bright yellow. He watched carefully as the three dots on the radar grew larger by the second until eventually he had visual contact.

He watched the Gyrospheres moving with infinite ease seemingly hovering yet moving all the time at a deceptive speed. He radioed the commander.

"Open mother ship - receiving compartment."

"Yes leader immediately" he eased his dart to the rear of number one command modules right hand Gyroscope. He edged gently to the massive golden support frame until he saw the docking doors open. Once they had fully opened he glided inside and descended to the landing pad. The doors then closed behind him, gently sliding until they had locked together.

Nepht stepped out onto a moving platform. This platform passed through all the main framework corridors surrounding both balancing Gyroscopes and led to all major areas in the Gyrophere including the central globular command area.

It was the first time Nepht had seen the Gyrosphere in full working order. He stood there in his proud pose glancing at each passing doorway. First he passed the engine room, then the computer bank. All around him he could hear the echoing sound of major gear changes in the complicated Gyrosphere system. The clear Perspex corridors allowed perfect viewing of the intricate machinery in operation. He felt like a tiny particle travelling through a vast clock.

The command module entrance was lit up in fluorescent purple. It had its own moving slipway leading off the platform. Nepht transferred over to the slipway on which he was carried straight to the automatic slide doors. They opened and he entered into a large circular chamber lit up in bright gold from the reflection of both adjacent Gyroscope stabilisers. Nepht, who was the only naked Sheerak, was received by the commander.

"We've heard about Salak's death." His tone was reassuring as if he was offering condolences. "What happened? Before Nepht could answer the commander noticed his wound. "Oh no," he said concerned "you have been injured also."

"I am fine" Nepht brushed off his concern. "What happened at the palace can be discussed another day. Now we have more pressing issues. Are the umbilical crafts in readiness?" He asked changing the subject.

"The pilots are briefed and in position." The commander said in a clear and powerful tone. "Once they hear the battle klaxon they will move to the Gyroscopes slip stream." He had got the message that now was not the time to discuss Salak's death but he knew that after this they would have to. Something about Nepht didn't seem right. He had always been struck by the tranquillity of the palace and often thought about how loyal the guards were. He just couldn't imagine them staging a coup. Nepht's naked scales made him suspicious too. Why would he remove Salak's uniform? These questions would have to wait but if Nepht thought he could hide in the moment of the battle and just walk into power he was mistaken. The commander knew something was wrong and he was sure others would share his view.

"We must position the Gyrospheres well apart for we don't want to make it too easy for the Tardan. We must also ensure that the darts are in a good location for they will give us added protection" Nepht instructed. "Radio both commanders of number two and number three Gyrospheres and tell them to keep well apart." Whilst speaking he looked up from his centralised control panel and saw the darts moving into position all around the transparent sphere.

"Good they are here also. Now we must wait. Commander, energise the computer radar screen."

The commander pulled a lever at the side of the control panel, a huge graphic screen lit up directly in front of them. Its white vertical and horizontal coordinates stood out perfectly against the muted blue background screen. Although the electronic fissure points at the extremities of each horizontal band were making erratic crackling sounds Nepht still seemed reasonably happy with its clarity.

"Give me the map," demanded Nepht, The commander carefully placed it into Nepht's claws,

"Let me see" pondered Nepht as he looked diligently at the map. The cross is well inside the Tardan land and according to our screen their battle fleet are getting near. He studied the map further. It's so detailed it must be authentic he thought. His razor sharp teeth were dripping with saliva which was ebbing down his gruesome features and falling onto the map. With a crude swipe from the back of his claw he wiped away the offending drips.

The central panel began to flash a brilliant orange on and off forcing Nepht to look at the screen.

The warning sign read; Action Imminent with the exact position of the Tardan craft showing on the digital map. They were perilously close.

"We should be getting visual contact any time now," said Nepht, trying to hide the sense of apprehension from his voice. He continued to deploy the umbilical craft. The commander pressed the alert klaxon and at this a series of floors located along the rear horizontal support frame of the Gyrospheres slid open revealing the small bullet shaped umbilical craft. This action was repeated in the other Gyrospheres. All operators then pressed release buttons and the umbilical craft began to gradually drift away from the main Gyrospheres attached to them with single lifeline cords. The cords enabled the umbilical craft to be operated anywhere within the slipstream of the Gyrosphere. They gave added fire power too for each of these small machines had been fitted with high power lasers. To assist their stability the pointed nose which faced towards the craft would cut through any turbulence that might occur.

"Contact!" said Nepht excitedly, adrenalin running through his thick scaled veins.

"There must be at least ten machines" exclaimed the commander.

The Sheerak stared and pondered the strange shape of their enemy's craft.

Nepht shook himself out of it aware that in war even a seconds delay could be fatal, "Open our frontal framework doors!" A succession of portholes slid open all along the front of each horizontal support frame revealing the attack lasers. "Send in the darts. Don't use the main Gyrosphere lasers until they are within range."

Six darts left their protective positions close to the Gyrosphere support frame and headed rapidly towards the Tardan Pendurotors. But as they did so, five Pendurotors dropped in altitude descending quickly to ground level. After some panic and confusion in the Sheerak crafts it became evident that the Tardan Pendurotors had re-emerged at the rear of the Sheerak Gyrospheres.

Wok and Revar had remained with the five frontal Pendurotors. Wok screamed spitting in excitement; "attack!" As the Tardan controllers attempted to lock lasers on to their scaly enemy they were struck by small but fierce battle projectiles that were fired from the Sheerak Darts .

These flying bullets were powerful weapons; they simultaneously hit number 5 Pendurotor ripping a huge hole in its outer shell. Rather than exploding, the heat of these lasers appeared to melt the metal of the Tardan craft which had been tested to withstand the heat of the Sheerak land and lasers but not both simultaneously. The Tardan machine was suddenly falling downwards lurching back and forth like a falling leaf until finally it exploded on impact in the dense undergrowth below.

"Did you see that!?" exclaimed Nepht salivating at the thought of all those Tardan deaths.

After striking the Pendurotor the six Sheerak darts swept round in a long sweeping arc and headed straight back towards the enemy craft but at different trajectories.

"Hit them with all we've got," shouted Wok so loud that his voice broke. The four remaining frontal Pendurotors let loose a hail of blinding beams instantly obliterating three of the incoming darts and badly damaging a fourth. The red fragments of the decimated darts fell to the forests below like tattered leaves being blown from a dying rose.

"Get back here quickly," said Nepht to the remaining two pilots. He then glanced to the rear of his Gyrosphere. He could see the Tardan crafts were edging closer all the time.

The pilots of the advancing Pendurotors were understandably cautious for they were wary of the unseen fire power of the Sheerak Gyrospheres.

The co-pilot of the Sheerak umbilical craft radioed Nepht with his scaly pincer hovering over the fire button "We await your instruction Sir."

"Hold fire" Nepht responded. "Let them get a little closer," his voice was quiet and reflective, it was clear he had a plan. "Spread out within the slip stream and try to gain as many different angles as you can."

The commander of the five approaching rear Tardan Pendurotors saw the Gyrosphere's umbilical craft moving into various positions, sensing they were preparing to strike he gave the order to open fire immediately. The Umbilical Craft were quick though and the laser fire went wayward flashing skyward into the yawning void of the tropical skies.

Wok and Revar's craft was still out of Nepht's firing range but was continuing its steady flow forward. Nepht sensed his chance and told the leader of the umbilical craft to fire at will towards the incoming Pendurotors to their rear. The laser fire flashed in from all angles at the unsuspecting Tardan formation. The two flanked Pendurotors were hit. Almost instantly one of them exploded into a galaxy of rainbow colours while the other was so badly damaged that it collided with the Pendurotor on its inside and the two of them spun to the ground locked together in a last turbulent dance of death.

Wok lurched forward at his control panel deeply alarmed at what he had seen.

"Return to position," he gasped feeling as if he was losing the ability to breathe. The two remaining rear positioned Pendurotors dropped altitude abruptly and performed a reverse manoeuvre back to the location of Wok.

"I'm glad we kept our frontal formation here." said Wok to Revar, "at least they will give us strong back up especially when the reinforcements arrive."

"Agreed," said Revar, "May I suggest that we divert one of our Pendurotors when Lato arrives to locate the area of Gux's map."

"Good idea" said Wok, "after all that's one of the reasons we are here ."

"We will soon be in the firing range of the Sheerak craft," Revar pointed out.

"Good let's try and surprise them again," said Wok hopefully. "Instruct three of our Pendurotors to veer off and hone in on the nearest Sheerak machine. If we destroy it we will even up the odds a little."

The three Pendurotors to the right of Wok's centralised position veered off on command. Their golden exterior shone brilliantly in the reflection of the mid-day sun flashing intermittently towards the on-looking Sheerak crew members, temporarily blinding them.

They swept in towards the Sheerak craft at high velocity completely surprising the enemy. Moments later they let rip a merciless barrage of laser fire. The glowing laser beams smashed into one of the Gyrosphere's with a tremendous force completely shearing through its main structure. Its right hand Gyroscope broke off amidst a terrible sound of wrenching steel and plummeted erratically to the forests below trailing its umbilical craft in its wake like a huge fiery streamer.

The other broken part consisting of the module sphere and another Gyroscope spun about wildly before it too broke up sending the two sections straight down. Whilst sweeping away after the successful attack the Tardan crew had been so close to the blast that they actually witnessed the spheres occupants falling around in disarray and panic.

"It could so easily have been us." Nepht said Gulping in anguish. Quickly recovering he added "activate our front lasers; we may catch the tails of their raiding craft."

The three Pendurotors sped back towards their battle positions next to Wok but two of them were caught in the hail of crossfire being unleashed from the remaining Sheerak Gyrospheres. At first the two Pendurotors that were hit seemed to steady themselves but then a massive explosion ripped through one of them sending red hot twisted metal careering through the white opaque shell of the other stricken craft forcing it into a lifeless vertical dive.

The pink Esterevanian sky was becoming totally blemished in silver and grey billowing smoke. The battle had swayed so far inland that the tropical heat was gradually carrying the lethal sulphuric fumes towards the Sheerak city. The dense forests below were becoming a scorched and fiery graveyard of tangled machinery and weapons.

Wok looked glumly down at the forest fires below him.

"Where are the reinforcements?" he muttered . Revar's smooth hand rested gently on his shoulder,

"Look they are approaching." Wok lifted his head quickly and stared through the view finder, his heart leapt with relief.

"I was beginning to think something had happened to them."

The Sheerak occupants shook their heads in disbelief. "Not more of them," cried Nepht allowing his dismay to show. He stroked his scales impatiently.

"Their leader is smart," he reflected. "Now he has the advantage against my two battle craft but hopefully my remaining darts can inflict a lot of damage before they re-group." He walked from the centralised control panel and up a narrow ramp to the circular walkway that surrounded the inside of the transparent command module. He looked once again at the distant enemy craft.

What will he do next? He thought.

"Nine of our battle darts are on their way to strike at the regrouping Tardan's." His commander said interrupting his thoughts. "This leaves six darts to protect our two remaining Gyrospheres."

Nepht studied the darts veering off into a pincer movement . He then turned and walked back down towards the control panel. The Tardan Pendurotor's were moving into position when Lato radioed Wok.

"I see there has been plenty of action. "Yes" said a hesitant Wok, " some machines have been destroyed already. The fighting has been quite fierce at times but hopefully we will overcome them now. It seems we have gained the upper hand . Remember one of the main objectives is to find those maps. Someone will have to break away from the main fleet and begin a search of the map area."

"I agree," said Lato on the radio "but whom?"

"I'll do it," said a sudden voice interrupting. It was Tak joining the conversation through the radio.

"I'm not sure," pondered Wok. "I could do with your skills here in battle"

"You have already said that our primary objective is to retrieve the maps" screamed Tak. Wok hesitated.

"Right, you're the one Tak, as soon as we start the next wave of fighting and the Sheerak are distracted split up from the task force and head straight to the destination marked on the maps."

Tak felt proud to have been given such an important responsibility. He was venturing in to the unknown, the first Noron to truly explore the Sheerak land.

"Action stations," he announced. "I want everyone on alert; we have an important mission ahead of us." Tak proceeded to brief his men but as he was speaking he noticed a formation of enemy craft on the radar. They were bearing in at great speed on both flanks of the re- forming Tardan battle formation.

"Attack coming in on both flanks, Wok do you receive?" he shouted.

"You leave now Tak," Wok ordered. "Break away," Tak pressed his underside thrusters and his Pendurotor lifted vertically from the formation almost colliding with the incoming Sheerak darts.

"Full velocity" ordered Tak as his Pendurotor engine gained speed. The Pendurotor surged forward veering away diagonally from the battle scene . He glanced down and was shocked to see Lato's Pendurotor blasted apart by the concentrated fire of the Sheerak darts. He watched dejectedly as the remainder of Lato's craft sprinkled lazily downwards. He turned away from the violent scene, deeply affected by what he had seen. Moments later he had recovered his composure and was directing the crew as usual. He studied the radar screen, the battlefield was only a tiny spot now. Nepht realised one of the Pendurotors was breaking away . He did the same . He wanted those maps too . Tak thought to himself "I must succeed for Lato's sake." As the time passed he felt increasingly psyched up.

"Look down Sir," said his assistant, "it must be the Sheerak city." Tak looked down and studied the sparkling towers below.

"Lower speed and altitude I want a better look. Activate the atmosphere sensors" he instructed.

The combined fragrance of fruit and flowers flooded through the sensor probes and into the chamber. He took a greedy inhalation. "It's certainly different from our pungent atmosphere."

Below them they could see the Sheerak people were gathering. They were staring upwards in curiosity at this strange craft.

"Lower us down to ground level." Said Tak. "I have an idea."

"Ground level?" questioned the startled assistant.

The Pendurotor gently glided down to a soft landing on the terrazzo surface of the main Sheerak square. The Sheerak people were lulled in and began to throng around the craft. They were clearly a fearless nation.

"Now activate the spike crushers." said Tak sternly trying to hide his wry smile. .

The assistant paused. He couldn't accept this as an actual option. Killing countless Sheerak was definitely not the solution but Tak didn't seem to appreciate that . Tak pressed a series of buttons on his control dashboard. As each button was pressed a corresponding light on the inner shell lit up until the whole interior was masked in multi coloured flashing lights.

"Now for ground rotation," said Tak as he activated the main pendulum.

At first the Pendurotor moved slowly causing no undue panic within the captivated Sheerak crowds. But as it started to roll faster, it suddenly dawned on the watching crowds what was happening and panic set in. The Pendurotor ploughed into the terrified Sheerak hoards at full speed, crushing all in its path. The individual spikes soon became clogged with impaled Sheerak bodies forcing Tak to slow down a little.

The Pendurotor moved in all directions following the fleeing crowds. Horrifying screams filled the tropical air as first the central speaking podium and then the magnificent city fountains were crushed and destroyed in systematic fashion.

Tak's assistant stared in disbelief at what was happening. He looked at Tak gleefully operating the controls like a man possessed. He was forced to turn away, feeling nothing but disgust. Tak pressed the deactivate sequence.

"This works perfectly" he announced smiling. But there was no reply. He surveyed the decimated square where only moments before there had been complete serenity. It was littered with Sheerak bodies and the once ornate terrazzo was reduced to a mass coffin. The marble statues lay crumbled in heaps being occasionally showered by the erratic spray of the broken fountains. Tak turned away from the carnage. He had a moment of horrifying clarity;

"I'm getting like Wok," he said to himself. He quickly shook off this unpleasant feeling, despite what he had just done. He rationalised that he couldn't be like Wok, he was Noron. He composed himself again before speaking to his operatives.

"Quite a success don't you think?" There was no roar of approval only a feeble response to his question. He could hear words like slaughter and murder being murmured in dissenting tones but he ignored the remarks. "Take off, we shall need to scan the map objective."

He pressed the spike retraction buttons and as each spike spun within its protective laser the impaled bodies on the tips dropped off gradually forming a circular heap of crumpled bodies on the terrazzo below the craft. Once the last spike had been retracted the order to take off was implemented. The Pendurotor rose silently and then sped off towards the Antovian ocean.

As they continued the journey Sheerak blood that had caked the spikes now oozed through the inner shell and ebbed down the brilliant white walls like a macabre art show. Everyone saw the blood but ignored it as if it were a silent, sick reminder of the cost of war.

News of the massacre had reached the Sheerak construction centre where a few personnel had remained to operate the essential computers. They dispatched a message to the troops on the outskirts of the city and before long they had transported ground attack lasers to the distant slopes of the Antovian beach head.

The fighting was getting closer to the peaceful Burabob territory. They were at this point blissfully unaware of the violence. The flying fish from Virejus were watching though and made haste to inform their king Lome.

CHAPTER 27

A STRANGE PHENOMENA

The only place that seemed quiet was the underground Tardan city where Orsov lay captive.

"Do you feel any pains yet?" He said gently to his pregnant wife.

"Not yet, I promise I will let you know when they start." She said, tenderly patting his fur reassuringly.

Rostia settled down reasonably well considering the circumstances; although she did occasionally scream Eli's name in her sleep. Thori consoled her each time by stroking her head. She never even woke properly but she was aware that she wasn't alone and this was a feeling she appreciated greatly.

"How do you think the battle is going?" Orsov asked Thori. "Do you think the Tardan can be victorious?"

The imprisoned leader sat slumped against the cell bars, he picked out bits of sawdust from his matted hairy arms and threw it onto the dusty floor.

"It's a hard question," he pondered. "Unlike our previous civil wars, this time, the enemy is unknown. All I know for sure is that I need to get out of this stinking hole."

"At least they put sawdust out for us," Orsov joked, always trying to lighten the mood. Thori didn't see the funny side; either that or he wasn't listening.

"I have been watching the guard change very carefully," Thori said in a hushed tone. "There doesn't seem to be a lot of guards on patrol. The time elapsing between guard changes is ample enough for us to slip away."

"That's all very well, said Orsov holding onto the cold steel bars, "but how do we get through these? Bite our way through?"

Once again Thori ignored Orsov's attempt at gallows humour. "I have been pondering a solution, but there isn't anything obvious" he said sombrely.

Suddenly both were distracted by a light tapping on the metal bars. They turned to see the Pico standing in the guard's entrance to the cells peering down at them.

"It's my helper," exclaimed Orsov excitedly. "Number Three," he had never been more pleased to see him.

"I have been looking for you," said Number Three plainly.

"Well, here I am," laughed Orsov, "bet you didn't expect to find me here."

"The probability was low Master," Number Three retorted.

"Are there any other guards out there?" Orsov questioned.

"No Master."

Suddenly Orsov realised he had a plan. He realised he had hope.

"Good, now listen carefully, go to my home as quickly as you can and fetch my spare hand laser. It will be lying under a floorboard under the rug in the main room. Do you understand?"

"Yes Master."

"Go now" Orsov ordered as he watched the Pico helper turn around and lumber out through the prison alleyway. All four of them waited in silence, they all knew this was their only chance of getting out and it seemed as if everyone was afraid to say or do anything in case they jeopardised it in some way. So they all stood there as if frozen to the spot.

Within 20 minutes the familiar sound of the Pico's steady footsteps could be heard approaching. They all looked at each other and allowed themselves a smile. He entered the alleyway with a large laser concealed between his huge fibred hands. Orsov jumped about excitedly. He passed it through the cell bars to the eager palms of his master.

"Thank you Number Three," Orsov gushed, "thank you so much. Now stand away from the bars and the rest of you get back," he gestured to those in the cell with him to stand against the wall.

With short sharp bursts of laser fire, Orsov began to cut through the steel bars of the cell until he had a big enough hole for them to crawl through. Erith chocked on the smoke from the laser gun bursts.

Orsov stood by his escapee exit like a proud father as his fellow captives made their way out before him. Just before it was Erith's turn she embraced her husband. "I am proud of you," she smiled.

"You should know me by now," he smiled cheekily. "Never let you down yet." He turned to Number Three in a more serious tone, "Go to the main perimeter roadway and if it is all clear, we shall follow."

"Yes Master." Number Three plodded slowly and deliberately towards the roadway, the group were in an obvious rush and each footstep of the Pico seemed to take an age.

"It's at times like this," Orsov said sarcastically, "I wish he could move a little faster." Thori looked at him with a smile but said nothing, this was still progress, it seemed like the glimmer of hope they now had was giving Thori a sense of humour again, all be it small.

"At least most of the city people are sleeping," Rostia said. She was right. This was the best possible time for them to travel. It seemed as if everything was going as it should and yet anxiety still lay thick in the air. They all looked cautiously towards the alleyway with nervous expressions. Suddenly a wry smile came over Orsov's face as he saw Number Three waving the all clear. They crept to the end of the gem studded alleyway; Orsov poked his small head out from behind the corner and checked the roadway again. There was no sign of life at all.

"Let's go," he said. "it's now or never."

They moved gingerly down the main road which was one of the most direct routes to the exit stairway. Occasionally they would take cover in doorways if they sensed movement ahead but fortunately it never amounted to anything.

"We've come this far, only a few steps now," whispered Orsov.

"What about transport? Erith will never make it through the ice formations," said Thori in a concerned voice.

Orsov shook his head, he had obviously thought of this, especially as it was his wife that was pregnant. He was shocked that a leader of a Tardan army had only just thought to ask this question. The strain of the day had obviously got to him.

"They always tie up their bear mounts at the entrance so we should be alright." Orsov replied, not hinting to Thori his personal dismay. "They only thing is, they normally have a guard looking after them." replied Orsov.

"I can take good care of any guards we meet," Thori said boldly. "It shouldn't be too difficult."

"I hope so," replied Erith who normally hates arrogance but in this case she was grateful for Thori's confidence.

"You lead the way Number Three,"

Orsov put his long arm around Erith, "I know it is a bit of a climb," he said quietly, "but we will take our time and we are all here to help you."

"Don't worry about me," said Erith dismissively, she knew he was being kind but she hated the thought of being a burden.

"It's alright Orsov," interrupted Thori. "I'll be behind her, just in case she stumbles."

Erith mentally shook her head, determined not to stumble.

Number Three led the way, closely followed by the others. It took ten very anxious minutes to climb the difficult terrain to the top platform.

At the top they sat down for a few moments to catch their breath. Orsov wiped the dripping sweat from his forehead and spoke breathlessly to the Pico.

"Open the latch and see if anyone is there, Remember now, open it gently, we don't want a guard to hear you."

Number Three reached up with both angular arms and gradually slid the door back until there was enough room for him to poke his head through. He was instantly blinded by the thick swirling snow but he persevered, straining his red robotic eyes as he looked for anything unusual. Then he lowered his head back inside again, a blanket of snow had come to rest on his large oval head.

"Don't tell me there's a blizzard blowing?" said Orsov despairingly.

"Ok," There was a pause.

"Is there a blizzard blowing?" asked Orsov laughing at Number Three's inability to take sarcasm.

"Yes Master."

Orsov contemplated this new complication, "we have to carry on he said, we have no other option. At least they won't be able to follow our tracks easily."

"Are the bear mounts there?" asked Thori.

"Yes," replied Number Three, "they are opposite the doorway."

"Let's move then."

The surge of adrenalin kept them all going in the face of immediate danger, Erith held her swollen belly and wished she wasn't pregnant which made her feel instantly guilty. It wasn't the baby Tardan she didn't want though; it was the fear of the world she was bringing the innocent life into. She knew she could start going into labour at any time and this thought alone left her feeling anxious. Not that she would let on to any of the males around her she felt this way; they wouldn't leave her alone if she did!

As they climbed through the entrance, Orsov thought he saw something small move at the mound behind the bear-mounts but he shrugged it off and kept going. The snow was at least a foot deep as they waded nervously towards the bears. Orsov lifted Erith and gently placed her on to the back of her own mount then glanced back through the snow fall just in time to see a shadowy figure move menacingly towards Thori.

Thori yelled out and lunged forward falling off his own mount and on to the sinister figure. They struggled about in the deep snow and for a moment, Orsov thought Thori was getting into difficulties but soon Thori managed to roll on top of his assailant, grasping his neck with both hands. He pressed both thumbs as far into the windpipe as he could. He squeezed until the struggling figure fell back in the snow, lifeless. Thori sat there astride his dead opponent staring into the driving snow but the biting cold awakened his wandering mind and brought him back to reality.

"That was close, Thori" said Orsov anxiously, but there was no reply from Thori. He just sat there, staring down dejectedly.

"What is it?" asked Orsov

"It's unfortunate that we are once again killing fellow Tardan It's insane, even as we fight our biggest enemy, we should be united, this is wrong."

"If you hadn't killed him, he would have killed you," Orsov reassured. "Let's just hope we don't encounter any more violence. We must leave now though."

Orsov snapped the reigns and his mount moved forward, head bowed into the blizzard .

For hours they trudged on and on; five tiny specks in a sea of ice and blinding snow until mercifully, the blizzard started easing.

As the snowing appeared to filter out and stop altogether, the travellers looked at each other, all of them beaming. They let out a cheer of relief and joy, waving their arms in the air to show their gratitude. Their echoed voices were a reminder of another disadvantage though; Orsov stared all around at the vast open ice terrain.

"Now that light is here again," Thori said in a warning tone, "we will be seen more easily. The journey ahead may now be physically easier but there are many dangers ahead."

"Hopefully that won't happen" said Rostia with a sense of jaded optimism.

"Always assess the risk from a realistic perspective," Thori scolded her. "There is no point blindly believing that everything will be OK, if we did that we wouldn't be looking for possible threats."

Rostia shook her head. She could spend hours arguing with Thori but she didn't have the energy. She was only trying to lift everyone, she didn't need a lecture.

Suddenly, an unexpected and unexplained faint buzzing sound could be heard in the distance. It grew louder and louder forcing the escape party to halt. They all looked skywards, anxiously waiting for something to come into view.

The noise it made was unique and it seemed to dawn on them all that this was potentially very bad news. A look of horror spread across their faces.

"That must be a Sheerak craft." Thori said what they were all afraid to. "It must have broken free from the fighting over the Tukas but why is it here?"

"The maps," Orsov exclaimed. "They are looking for those blasted maps; we are doomed."

He dismounted and clutched Erith from her saddle. The others dismounted too. They gathered in a small circle, putting their bear mounts to the outside, in a last desperate act of defence waiting in a pathetic huddle to be cut to pieces.

The Gyrosphere moved closer and closer with Nepht at the controls. He had pin-pointed the crouched figures through his infra-red system. Even more ominous was the fact that he was in no mood to take any prisoners. His mind was still on the battle he had just left . But his greed was guiding him to the maps, even though he knew the battle was still undecided . He prodded at his seeping wounds gently trying to close the gaping cut.

"Look at them," he mocked. "They are weak and unworthy of life. I will exterminate them." Nepht took pleasure in the fear the Tardan group were displaying. He would end their pitiful misery soon. He pressed the infra-red lock on sequence and held his claw over the activation button.

Suddenly he felt a strange vibration shake his whole body. He just had enough time to turn round and see his crew being struck too. His mouth locked into a disbelieving expression then his mind went blank. The entire crew and their mercenary leader stood motionless. The Gyrosphere seemed to be overtaken by strange phenomena; it gently landed on the ice below without any intervention from the Sheerak occupants.

The Tardan group who had been holding their breath heaved a sigh of relief. They still had no idea what was going to happen next but they were all surprised to still be alive at all.

"They've landed," said Orsov puzzled. "Maybe they are friendly after all!"

They slowly picked themselves up from their huddled position and warily made their way over to the huge gleaming craft.

"Look at the size of it," muttered Orsov. "That must be the stabilisers," he said pointing to the twin Gyroscopes.

"It must be 50 metres across," said Thori in amazement. Suddenly, as he spoke, an entrance slid open. They all froze, waiting for a Sheerak figure to make an entrance on to Tardan soil.

They waited.

Nothing happened.

"Do you think its Sheerak custom that we go inside? asked Rostia. "It might be a trap."

"Well we can't stand here forever," Orsov Joked.

"Let's do it then," Erith said taking a step forward. Orsov was quick to jump in front of his pregnant wife and led the way on board the mystery alien craft. The small group edged their way up the steep golden entrance platform, staring inside for any sign of life. As they neared the main sphere, the strong heat from inside buffeted against the matted snow on their faces and bearskins, bringing with it an immediate thaw.

"I didn't know our bodies would even withstand this level of heat?" Thori queried. They were all excruciatingly hot but their bodies were functioning ok, or at least as far as they could tell. They cautiously edged their way in to the main common chamber looking all around as they did so. Upon reaching inside disbelief spread over their faces. A few moments passed before they could even speak to each other.

Orsov broke the silence. "Look at them, they seem to be mummified."

"I wonder if they can speak?" enquired Thori. "Both he and Orsov looked at each other silently daring each other to move first. Gradually they both tiptoed towards the lifeless crew members. Orsov stood in front of one who was naked standing upright by his controls; he was facing the rest of the crew but looked like he had been frozen in mid turn as his body was still partly facing towards the controls. He reached out and touched the glistening scales on the large reptilian body but there was no reaction.

They were so tall that to see into their yellow deep set eyes, Orsov had to bring over a swivel chair from the doorway. He stood on it, bringing him up to eye level with the Skeerak figure. He moved his small hairy hand in front of the Sheerak's eyes causing a momentary flicker but then nothing. He looked over to Thori who was inspecting the creature's wounds.

"They are alive alright, but all intelligent functions seem to be missing, it's like a living shell." Orsov looked again at the grotesque features. He ran his finger nail along the protruding serrated teeth and paused again to stare at the eerie lifeless eyes.

"It gives me the shivers being this close. I am glad I don't have to fight him."

During this inspection Erith and Rostia had remained by the doorway, too frightened to move.

Orsov looked at them. "It's OK, there is no danger. Look I can even make him move." Orsov pulled at the Sheerak's gruesome pincers with both hands forcing the mummy to walk a few faltering steps. Suddenly the entrance door slammed shut forcing the females to jump inside.

What happened? Thori said startled.

"I don't know but I am going to find out," said Orsov anxiously. He moved towards the control panel in the centre of the sphere, pushing his fists hard into the floor to get momentum. As he neared the panel a strange relaxed feeling came over him.

The other three Tardan also felt the same; the only one still able to move unaffected was Pico. They became transfixed in a deep hypnotic state, gradually they all sat down. It was a strange sensation, they didn't feel completely disconnected from each other or physically trapped, just relaxed, peaceful and calm. Orsov was even able to move his arm around Erith and smile. For the first time in a life time, they each actually experienced a feeling of contentment.

They had all lived through conflict and had become used to being on constant high alert, ready for the next battle. In this moment though, they experienced something new. As they sat aboard an alien ship they all knew that some kind of divine power was controlling them, they were no longer scared. For the first time in their existence, they knew they were safe and loved and that was all that mattered.

After a moment of tranquillity, the Gyrosphere's controls lit up and began to activate. There was a slight jolt forward before the ship lifted skyward and veered off.

Destination unknown.

CHAPTER 28

THE AWAKENING

Lome, the Virejus leader sat at a great coral conference table in the amphitheatre of thought. He was surrounded by his trusted aides. The clear warm waters of their underwater domain were perfectly still as Lome spoke.

"Our flying fish have done well; their information about the turmoil on Esterevania has forced us into action. There will be no violence anymore. Never again will we allow hatred to infest those that live in this great land. Our intervention has been very effective. The battle over the Tuka mountains has completely stopped and the slaughter near the Antovian beach head has also ceased. The Gyrosphere with Orsov aboard will land soon on the beach and we will be there to greet him.

The Gyrosphere drifted gradually towards the Antovian beach. Its twin gyroscopes spun rapidly throwing out shafts of reflected sunlight as the ship momentarily eclipsed above the surface entrance to the Burabob crab home. Orsov rubbed his eyes and continued to stare peacefully into space.

He gradually became more aware of his surroundings. He realised they were landing on a beach. He turned to look at his beautiful wife and was struck with how much love he had for her. He had always known this of course, but now, for some reason unbeknown to him, he was overwhelmed by it.

"Do you feel alright?" he asked her. She simply rested her small head on his shoulders and sighed with a relaxing smile.

"What happened?" she asked calmly.

"I don't know but I know we are safe."

Thori and Rostia were stirring too. Direct sunlight was beginning to flood the transparent sphere, making Orsov feel a little hot. He found he was able to comfortably stand; he walked over to the viewing platform and looked over in disbelief. The view he saw was completely stunning he tried to speak but the words failed to come.

"What is it Orsov?" Thori asked. There was no reply so Thori joined Orsov to see for himself. He too was taken aback. "Come here, you have to see this," he gestured to the other two.

"The soil is pure white; it stretches as far as the eye can see. I have never seen anything like it before." Said Rostia

"Look at the water it is crystal clear." Erith added.

The door slid open and direct sunlight broke through. The Tardan's all automatically recoiled; they had been previously convinced that they would die after exposure to such heat. The atmospheric sense of peace relaxed them and stopped them from panicking. The sensation was strange, their thick fur felt heavier as it began to fill with sweat but they were still alive.

In the distance they could see strange figures coming towards them. Again considering the violent nature of their world they should have been anxious but none of them felt anything but love and peace. Before they could make out who the figures were they could hear a calming voice speaking to them. "Welcome to the beach," it said. "Come, step on to the sand."

Tentatively they all took their first steps out from the alien spacecraft on to this strange new world. They looked at each other bathed in sunlight and closely examined their furry hands which were covered in glistening sweat. It was hard to believe that just a few short hours before they had been in a blizzard and before that a prison. The sand was soft and hot under the pads of their feet. Extremes of *Iced Fire* became apparent .

"I am Lome," the divine voice spoke. The figures were getting closer now but still not close enough for the Tardan's to see clearly. Strangely though, it sounded as if the voice was softly whispering in their ear.

"Is it you that has caused the Sheerak to stop? Did you put them in that transfixed state?" Thori asked out loud.

"Yes" admitted Lome. "That was me."

"Why, what is going on?" Orsov asked. He was curious though, not scared.

"I've simply had enough of the violence; I have saved those of you who have peace in their heart. Do not worry the others will not be harmed. They will remain in a transient state until their souls accept peace. Your friends and your enemies will be kept safe."

At that moment, the figures came into view. A white intense light seemed to radiate from the figure at the centre of them .The group of white haired beings who were accompanying Lome stepped forward to greet Thori's group . And alongside them were the Burabob crab people including Ba Ba and Gux. Standing with them was one Sheerak, Grapite. The central figure stepped forward; they all knew it was Lome.

"You are safe now, it is all over. There will be no more fighting."

Orsov felt overcome with emotion as he gripped the partly hidden hand of Lome. A loud high pitched squeal of approval came from the watching Burabob, making Orsov turn to face them.

"Ah the crab race – so you are the people who brought us the map?" he looked along the cluster of Burabob until finally his eyes fell upon a frail old man.

"Why it's Tekir, Eli's friend. You are safe too."

"Yes Orsov though how I got here is a mystery to me", another person emerged through the cluster of Burabob, he was a Noron from the Tardan Empire.

He walked straight to where Rostia stood with Thori. Rostia was bemused by his actions and looked at Thori with a puzzled expression.

"You don't know me, but I have spent my life watching you grow up," he said. Rostia was even more confused.

"I know this will be hard for you to believe, but I am your father." Rostia staggered back into Thori's arms completely astonished.

"But I thought that mating was impossible for Noron."

"That was true in the beginning, but over the generations there has been a change in our genetic functions. I can only compare it with the self-initiated protective function of the Pico." Rostia walked to her Noron father's side and began to sob.

"So that is why my mother always kept quiet when I asked her about my parentage," she finally said through the tears.

"Yes probably. You see, Rostia we fell in love too. Just like you and Eli. Maybe the rebellious streak was passed on to you through us. I had to keep my distance though, cross breeding of any sort was illegal and your life would have been in danger if the authorities had found out. Because we loved you so much, your mother and I stayed apart."

Thori kept his head down in shame. He was part of the authority that saw cross breading as wrong; he was also the enabler of war. Lome reached out and put a gentle hand on Thori's shoulder, no words were spoken but the reassurance was loud and clear. Thori had been forgiven. His heart was peaceful now and that was all that mattered .

Rostia stood still holding her father's hand. Quietly content that another burning question had been answered in her mind. It also answered a long standing question for Orsov.

"Now we know where your intelligence comes from. I've pondered over it many times since our discussion about the vacuum probe. I thought of every possible answer but I must admit not this."

Lome looked at Rostia kindly, "your father is here because, like you, he is a pacifist."

"I suppose Tak, Revar and Wok have been incapacitated too?" Asked Orsov.

"Yes, it had to be," replied Lome. "Especially in Tak's case, towards the end he was becoming quite the degenerate."

For a few moments Orsov was lost in thought about the past. He remembered the great machines that had been built and all the camaraderie that went with it. What a waste he thought, what a waste.

The sound of pounding waves became even more apparent as the conversation hit a lull then Orsov spoke again.

"I still don't understand," he said. "Why does our fight concern you so much, who are you?"

"I have existed for longer than all the creatures on this planet. I have watched the world tear it-self apart for too long. I can no longer sit as a passive observer. It had come the time to act." The whole beach was listening intently. "I was not prepared to watch anymore innocents die."

Orsov looked at his pregnant wife and thought back to the moment when he held her, huddled in the snow, waiting for death at the hands of his reptile enemy. If Lome hadn't intervened Orsov and his small but beautiful family would have been killed.

"I must add," said Lome breaking Orsov's thoughts, "You were right, that giant intergalactic spaceship your people were told about at the treaty, was really there. It is how I travelled to this world. Of course there was no life here then. Through the power of Kuba I was able to breathe life into this planet. It is why I cannot see it destroyed."

The whole beach was silent. This was a huge revelation. Lome, this mystical creature was from another world and had given life to all of them through the divinity of Kuba.

They were stunned. The only sound to be heard was the lapping waves before Lome suddenly started to laugh; a warm and welcoming laugh, a laugh full of love and passion for life. Everyone around him couldn't help but join in until each person on the beach was roaring with laughter too.

"One more thing," Lome interrupted as the joyous sound died down, "the maps."

Thori and Orsov looked at each other and smiled. They had both completely forgotten about them.

"I have decided to reward you for all the strife you have endured. Here take this. It is the real map, giving you the perfect co-ordinates to the treasures of Esterevania, its from Kuba .

"You can follow them but your reward is to be spread out to all peaceful beings on this planet. Wealth was never meant to be hoarded but instead, shared."

"What about the maps Gux brought to us?" asked Orsov.

"They were false I had to find out who really wanted peace so we created the situation."

"It was such an elaborate plan but it is a fact that the true colours of someone will always be revealed during difficult times". They all understood Lome's methods.

"When you have finished your expedition you are welcome to live with me or return to your native homes. In all locations there are those who are free. Creatures filled with goodness are everywhere it is just a shame that the individuals consumed by hatred have had such an impact on your past. Now though, is the time to look to the future."

The group looked at each other unsure how to answer. It was all so much to take in .

"Don't worry now," Lome said kindly. "There are no restrictions to your life anymore."

They all bowed and thanked Lome as they headed towards the Sheerak craft, The Tardan four, Pico and Rostia's Noron father climbed upon the entrance ramp.

Grapite, stepped forward from the Crab folk and joined them also. Rostia's father put a protective arm around her saying " Now we will make up for all the lost time ." Gux waved goodbye content that he was now in the presence of Lome forever . There was no fear, for the first time in history all creatures stood side by side, all because of divine intervention.

As they spun off into the unknown on the Sheerak craft they held each other's hands.

This was a new world.

A new Esterevania .

Printed in the United States
By Bookmasters